# SHIPWRECKS

AKIRA YOSHIMURA

SHIPWRECKS

Translated from the Japanese
by Mark Ealey

*Harcourt Brace & Company*

NEW YORK   SAN DIEGO   LONDON

*Hasen* by Akira Yoshimura
© 1982 by Akira Yoshimura
Original Japanese edition published by Chikuma Shobo
English translation rights arranged with Akira Yoshimura
through Writer's House, Inc./Japan Foreign-Rights Center
English translation copyright © 1996 by Mark Ealey

Requests for permission to make copies
of any part of the work should be mailed to:
Permissions Department, Harcourt Brace & Company,
6277 Sea Harbor Drive, Orlando, Florida 32887-6777.

Library of Congress Cataloging-in-Publication Data
Yoshimura, Akira, 1927–
[Hasen. English]
Shipwrecks/Akira Yoshimura; translated from the Japanese
by Mark Ealey.—1st ed.
p.    cm.
ISBN 0-15-100211-8
1. Yoshimura, Akira, 1927–      —Translations into English.
I. Ealey, Mark.   II. Title.
PL865.072H3313   1996
895.6'35—dc20    95-40514

Text set in Goudy
Designed by Lori J. McThomas
Printed in the United States of America
First edition
A B C D E

# SHIPWRECKS

1

Old conical hats made of sedge moved in the line of surf. Spray shot up from the breakers, first at the end of the reef-lined shore, and then closer and closer as the waves rushed in, until the water where Isaku was standing swelled up and smashed onto the rocks before streaming back out again.

The surface of the water was foaming white from the fierce rain. A mixture of raindrops and spume from the waves trickled down through the holes in Isaku's hat. There was only a sliver of sandy beach on this rockbound coast, and there, too, people in sedge hats were busy collecting pieces of driftwood.

Isaku waited for a wave to subside, then stepped into the water and grabbed a piece of driftwood stuck between two rocks. Judging from its gentle arc and the nailhole-like depressions, there was no doubt that it was from a wrecked ship. It was too tightly wedged in for him, a mere boy of nine, to dislodge easily, but when he planted his foot firmly against one of the rocks and pulled, the wood started to come free.

Isaku scurried back to shore when he saw the next wave surge in, hurling spray into the air. He heard it breaking behind him, and seawater rained noisily onto his hat. When the wave subsided and began to flow back toward the sea, he stepped into the frothing water and grasped the piece of driftwood again.

After several attempts, he managed to work the driftwood in closer until a big wave finally washed it ashore. He hung on to it to avoid being carried away by the next wave. Digging his fingers into the depressions in the wood, he pulled it toward the path to the village.

Pelted by the rain, people carried bundles of wood on their backs up the path. The timber Isaku was pulling was considerably larger than theirs, and looked to be of firm, good quality. It seemed a shame to use it for burning a corpse when it could be used as firewood at home.

When Isaku reached the path, a woman wearing a sedge hat emerged from the house of the bereaved family and helped him with his load. They pulled it into the house and put it beside a rough pile of wood on the dirt floor of the lower section of the room.

He untied his hat and sat down on the woodpile, glancing across the room. The deceased was an old man, over fifty, named Kinzo. His body was naked except for a loincloth. When Kinzo had become too sick to move, he had lost his appetite, and for the last few days his family had been giving him nothing but water. Nobody would feed those judged certain to die.

Dead people due to be placed in a sitting coffin were tied seated with their back to a funeral post, their legs bent at the knees and then tightly bound with rough straw rope before rigor mortis could set in. Kinzo's bones jutted out beneath his skin; his abdomen was distended and taut. His head hung down and slightly forward, revealing the hemp stalk tied to a cross placed on the thin gray hair of his topknot to ward off demons.

Isaku's mother was wiping down the coffin that sat on the floor. A large pot of vegetable porridge, provided by the people of the village, simmered away on the fire, the smell wafting down to the dirt floor.

The downpour seemed to intensify. The noise of the waves faded as the house was enveloped in the sound of the rain.

Isaku gazed at the woman's hand stirring the porridge with a ladle.

The next morning the rain stopped and a typical clear autumn sky unfolded.

People emerged from their houses and gathered at the home of the bereaved family. Inside, the old women of the village chanted sutras in hushed voices.

Isaku left Kinzo's house carrying a bundle of chopped driftwood on his back. He joined men lugging unwieldy bundles of sticks and twigs on their backs up the narrow village path onto the trail that led to the mountain pass.

The mountain's rugged face, flecked with bare rocks, loomed behind the village. The seventeen little houses seemed to be clinging to the narrow coastline so as not to be pushed down into the sea. Perhaps because of the constant exposure to the salty winds off the sea, the wooden walls of the houses were white, as if dusted with powder. The thatched roofs were weighted down against the wind with stones similarly blanched. Around the houses, on the more gently sloped land, there was a terraced field. Even with manure, the stony soil could yield only the meagerest of crops, nothing more than a few simple varieties of millet.

Isaku followed the men off the path into the forest. The ground was damp from the rain and there was an occasional puddle; at times he struggled to get his footing. Finally the trees thinned out and they came to a clearing in front of a line of small headstones and old wooden grave tablets. The men set down their bundles of firewood and dry branches near the three-sided stone crematory at one corner of the clearing.

Isaku sat down on a rock near the men. Sweat dripped from his brow and down his neck but felt good in the sea breeze. He looked down at his pile of wood.

The long, thin funeral procession moved away from Kinzo's house along the village path near the waterside. At its head a long white cloth fluttered on the end of a bamboo rod; next came the coffin, suspended from a thick pole. Children walked at the end of the procession.

"I don't want to be left for dead like him," whispered one of the men.

Kinzo had been laid up at home since summer. One day he had lost his footing and slammed his back against a rock while out spearing octopus on the reef. Unable to work, he became a burden on his family. In a village flirting with starvation, an invalid would be written off for dead.

People would grieve for a short while, but as they believed in reincarnation they quickly reconciled themselves to loss. Life was entrusted to humans by the gods, and upon death a person's spirit departed for a far-off place beyond the seas, but after a time it would return to the village, to take shelter in a woman's womb and come back in the form of an infant. Death was merely a period of deep sleep until the return of the spirit; excessive mourning would disturb the dead person's repose. The headstones and the wooden grave tablets faced the sea to guide the spirits home.

The funeral procession slowed when it reached the mountain trail.

As he watched the procession, Isaku thought of his father. That spring his father had been sold for three years of indentured service to a shipping agent at a southern port frequently visited by ships on the east-west run. His father went willingly and was undoubtedly now working on the boats. It seemed that his father had made up his mind to become indentured at the end of the previous year when another baby girl was born, joining Isaku, the eldest, his younger brother Isokichi and sister Kane.

He had heard that in other places people killed their newborns, but not in this village. A pregnancy meant the spirit of a dead person had returned to the village, and infanticide was unthinkable, even if the family risked starvation.

On several occasions, Isaku had seen his father's body moving rhythmically on top of his mother at night, in the semidarkness of their room, her splayed legs bending at the knees then thrusting out straight. He knew that they were urging the spirits of his ancestors to return, but he also knew that another child would further impoverish the family.

The village was bordered on the south by the cliffs of a cape which jutted out sharply into the sea. The only path to the outside world was the trail to the north along the mountain pass. The path was steep and rocky, traversing two deep gorges and then ascending up an almost sheer slope through a thicket of trees and vines. The village owed its isolation to the terrain. The villagers followed this path to other villages to exchange seafood for farm produce and the like. But this was never enough to satisfy their hunger.

A simple method of saving one's family from starvation

was indentured servitude. In the next village beyond the pass there was a salt merchant who doubled as a labor contractor. He would pay a lump sum as a bond for service. The family would use this money to buy grain to take back home to the village.

Mostly daughters were sold, but sometimes even the head of a family would sell himself. A fourteen-year-old girl called Tatsu had left the village at the same time as Isaku's father, to enter into a ten-year term of bondage in return for sixty silver *momme*, but his father was given the same payment for a three-year term, to all eyes an unusually favorable arrangement. His father was noted in the village for his sturdy build, and was an expert helmsman as well.

"I'll be back in three years. Don't let the children starve while I'm away."

Isaku's father had looked intently at him and his mother in the doorway of the broker's office.

His mother had bought some grain with part of the money, and carrying this on their backs they had set off along the mountain path toward the village. He was in awe of his father for receiving so much silver and wished for an admirable physique like his.

The men pausing to rest in the graveyard had all sold sons or daughters into bondage. The previous autumn, the frail man sitting next to Isaku had sold his wife for five years. The men who had carried the firewood and branches up to the graveyard and the four pallbearers were the only remaining male heads of households in the village.

On seeing the front of the line of people enter the forest, the men slowly stood up. They smoothed out the ashes left in the crematory and removed the dirt and ash blocking the draft holes in its stone walls. Untying the ropes around the bundles of dry branches, they placed the wood in parallel crosses inside the walls.

They could hear the sound of a bell. The procession was drawing closer to the middle of the forest. Isaku's mother carried the bamboo rod with the white cloth under her arm and held it high as they emerged from the trees. Behind the aged man sounding the bell came the old women, chanting the sutras. Then the coffin swayed into view. Isaku's mother stuck the rod into the ground and the coffin was placed beside the crematory. The pallbearers sat down here and there, opening their shirts and wiping the sweat from their brows. The men who had prepared the pyre released the coffin from the pole used to carry it up, and lifted it onto the pyre. Following the men's instructions, Isaku slipped pieces of firewood in between the gaps in the branches.

Smoke poured forth after the lighted hemp stalk was dropped onto the tinder and soon the branches began to burn. Those seated rose to their feet and stood around the stone walls. The bell was sounded, and again the sutras were recited.

As the crisscrossed pile of wood caught fire, the coffin was enveloped in flames. The sea breeze made the flames dance; they sounded like a cloth flapping in the wind. Sparks flew every time the wood cracked.

Isaku and the men had soaked some straw mats in a nearby stream, and now they threw them up on top of the pyre, smothering the flames to ensure that the body burned well. The coffin crumbled in the fire and colorful flames started to shoot out of the exposed corpse. Just when he thought he saw flames a dazzling yellow, they would change and flicker green. More firewood was stoked and wet mats were again thrown on top.

When the body had become quite small, toasted dumplings

made of millet were passed around. Isaku chewed away as he stared into the blaze. Tiny multicolored flames spurted forth when the men poked sticks roughly at the charred corpse. After they had done this several times the fire died down, and the body turned the bright red of burning charcoal.

The sun began to set.

Kinzo's family would spend the night under a canopy of straw mats strung up in the trees at the edge of the forest; the next morning they would recover the bones. The villagers pressed their hands together in prayer and then left the clearing.

Isaku trailed his sturdily built mother down the path through the forest. He had been struck by her repeatedly in the past. She was surprisingly powerful, and sometimes her blows left him temporarily deaf in one ear. She hit him for various reasons, but usually it was for being lazy. "Just look at the fish!" she would scold him. "They don't slack off." She was a frightening figure, but at the same time he also felt a kind of security knowing that he could rely completely on this mother who would beat him mercilessly.

They made their way through the forest and onto the mountain path. The scene was bathed in the afternoon sunlight, and the sea glistened. They could see crows circling above the little cape.

His mother chatted with the old women as they trudged the path. Isaku was happy; for the first time he had helped the men carry firewood up to the crematory for a funeral. He was being treated as an adult; before long he would be carrying the coffin with the men. But he was small for his age and slight of build. His father was due to return in two and a half years, and like other teenage boys and girls in the village Isaku would no doubt be sent into bondage in his father's

place, pretending to be two or three years older than he actually was. At such time, if he was small, the broker either
would refuse to barter for him would or take him on for a
paltry amount.

As he usually did, Isaku tiptoed down the path, trying to
appear taller. The women walking in front of him came to a
halt, and the villagers behind them also stopped. As one they
looked to the left. Isaku did the same.

In the distance, between two low mountains with bare
rocky faces, he could see a green-mantled ridge. "The mountains have started to turn red," whispered the old woman
beside him.

The ridges glimmered in the setting sun, but the top of
one ridge, towering conspicuously above the others, appeared
to be a light shade of washed-out red. Two days of rain had
kept the crest shrouded in mist, but during that time the trees
must have begun turning red. Isaku gazed at the ridge.

Every year the autumn color appeared on that crest first,
steadily spreading to other ridges and then gathering speed
like an avalanche, dyeing the surface of the mountain red as
it advanced downward. It would traverse the deeply chiseled
valleys, envelop the hills, and soon color the mountains behind the village. By the time this happened the yellowish
brown of leaves about to fall could be seen unfolding on the
more distant ridges.

In the village the feeling of autumn was thick in the air.
When the eulalia grass came into ear the men would start
catching the little autumn octopuses as they came closer to
shore. These were a delicacy that could be eaten either raw
or boiled. In most families the children would salt and dry
them, cutting them in half and hanging them up on strings
from poles.

The leaves would change to their autumn hues after these little octopuses appeared, and the villagers would be filled with anticipation at the sight of the red-tinted mountains.

The sea would become rough when the autumn colors faded and the leaves would begin to fall. If there were two days of calm, the next few days would be marked by angry, surging seas and spray from the waves raining down on the houses. But sometimes the rough seas would bring unexpected blessings, so much more bountiful than anything from the beach or the barren fields that no one would have to be sold into bondage for years. Such manna was all too rare, but the people lived in constant hope. The autumn colors heralded the time when the village might be visited by this good fortune.

The line of people moved along, their eyes still turned toward the top of the ridge. Isaku looked at the sea as he walked down the path. At low tide the rocks at the bottom of the sharply jutting promontory were exposed, and down in front of the village, set back ever so slightly from the sea, the tips of rocks could be seen projecting out of the foaming water.

The sea near the coast masked an intricate stretch of reef—home for octopus and shellfish, a haven for fish. Seaweed swayed back and forth and kelp lay thickly plastered against the rocks. The men fished in small boats while the women and children picked seaweed from among the rocks and gathered shellfish. The sea around the reef was not only a precious fishing ground which sustained the village, it was also a source of such luxuries as food, money, clothing, and daily utensils. But such bounty might come for two or three years in succession and then not for another ten. The most recent visitation had been at the beginning of winter six years earlier, when Isaku was three years old.

His memory of his early childhood days was rather dim, but he could vividly remember that incident. Everyone in the house had been unusually cheerful. His parents and all the other people in the village had been grinning, their cheeks flushed red with excitement. He remembered that the strange atmosphere had frightened him so much that he cried.

It was two years ago that he had learned the reason behind the excitement in the village.

As was the custom, when the autumn colors arrived the whole village took part in a ceremony that mystified Isaku. He asked a boy his age named Sahei what it was about.

"You don't know?" Sahei said, looking at him contemptuously.

Feeling ashamed, Isaku asked his mother when he got home.

"*O-fune-sama*," she replied.

Isaku looked perplexed.

"Look, that bowl there, that's from *O-fune-sama*," his mother said with obvious irritation as she glanced toward the shelf.

He looked at the bowl in a new light. It was different from rough-cut bowls that had merely been hollowed out of pieces of wood. This bowl was almost waferlike and of uniform thickness. It looked as though it had been lacquered in some way; the red surface of the wood had a shiny gloss to it, and two fine gold-colored lines were drawn just below the lip. This bowl was used only to hold food placed before the ancestral tablets at New Year and the Bon festival; otherwise, it never left the shelf.

His mother said nothing more.

He had no idea what link there was between the bowl and the village ritual, and it was Sahei, who had earlier derided him for his ignorance, who told him about *O-fune-sama* and the significance of the wooden bowl.

Sahei told him that *O-fune-sama* referred to the ships that were wrecked on the reef which stretched out in front of the village. These ships normally carried such things as food, utensils, luxury goods, and cloth, which would substantially improve the lives of the villagers. Also, pieces of ship's timber smashed by the rocks and angry seas and hurled up on the beach would be used to repair houses, or even to make furniture. The late-autumn village ritual was carried out in the hope that passing ships would founder on the reef.

"So you wouldn't know about the cave on Crow Beach, either, then?" Sahei said condescendingly as he turned his rheumy eyes toward the south. There was the little cape jutting out into the sea, defined by the white spray of the waves. Often crows could be seen circling in the sky above the several small pine trees standing atop the cape.

"I've heard about the cave. You mean the place where they throw the bodies washed up on the beach," said Isaku aggressively.

"Not just the ones that are washed up. It's also where they throw the bodies of the crew aboard *O-fune-sama*," said Sahei with a smirk on his face.

Isaku struggled to make sense of what Sahei said, though he grasped the significance of the ritual and the lacquered bowl.

He mused afresh over his memories from when he was three years old. It finally dawned on him that his father, mother, and all the other villagers had been in such high spirits because *O-fune-sama* had come that year. He recalled that for the next couple of years he had eaten foods unthinkable nowadays and had set eyes on all sorts of remarkable objects.

On festive occasions, or when there had been a death in the village, his mother would scoop rice from an earthenware pot and make him some gruel. When he had a fever she would bring out a jar ever so carefully and let him lick some white substance off her finger. This amazingly sweet powder, called white sugar, was also said to be effective in curing all ailments.

The light of the candle he saw at night at the Bon festival was likewise etched into his memory. It had been a gray color, shaped like a thin rod almost three inches in length, and he remembered his amazement when the wick had been lit. It was so incredibly bright that he was dazzled by the glare. How could such a little stick generate so much light? Besides, unlike pine torches and wicks soaked in fish oil, it did not give off any black smoke, and the smell was quite pleasant. It had a beautiful glow, at times crackling ever so slightly, sending tiny beads of light flying.

These two were undoubtedly part of the bounty from O-fune-sama, but before too long they were gone.

Even so, vestiges of previous good fortune were still present. The old mat on the floor next door, the chest in the village head's house carrying the insignia of a shipping company. Also, some households had the ship's large wooden fire buckets. It was now clear that like the lacquered bowl in Isaku's house, these were all from O-fune-sama.

2

Realizing that autumn was fast clos-
ing in on the village, Isaku stared at the red hues unfolding
on the far-off crests of the ridges through different eyes from
the previous year. Though he was happy at being allowed to
work alongside the men at the cremation, he was also aware
of his position in this village made up mostly of old people,
women, and children. Until this year, as a child, Isaku had
only watched village rituals, but from now on, he thought,
he, too, would have to take an active part in the proceedings.

After the cremation, the villagers all disappeared into
their houses. Isaku followed his mother into their house past
the straw mat hanging down at the doorway.

His sister Teru, born at the end of the previous year, was
on all fours and crying on the floor. She seemed to have been
crying for quite some time; her voice was hoarse. She crawled
toward them when she recognized her mother.

His mother ignored her and headed to the urn in the dirt
floor part of the house and scooped up some water with a

cracked bowl, gulping it down noisily before going into the outhouse at the back. By and by she reappeared, stepping up onto the matted floor and adjusting the bottom of her kimono. She sat down, casually positioning Teru on her knee. She opened her kimono to expose a large dark nipple.

Teru moved her head from side to side impatiently as she tried to latch on to the nipple. Isaku could hear Teru feeding; she seemed to have a stuffy nose. At times she would turn her head away from her mother and breathe so heavily she sounded like an adult.

It was the custom in the village to refrain from working both on the day of bereavement and on the day of the cremation so as not to disturb the dead. Isaku felt at ease, glad that he didn't have to go out fishing; at the same time, he feared his mother, knowing how she hated idleness. He cast furtive glances in her direction as he sat down on the edge of his bed.

There was no sign of his little brother and sister; he guessed they were playing in the woods behind the house. Faint wisps of purple smoke drifted up from the wood among the ashes in the fireplace.

"The mountains have turned red," Isaku said ingratiatingly to his mother.

She didn't reply. The afternoon sun shone in through a knothole in the wooden wall, throwing a single beam of light across the murk of the room onto the back of Teru's slightly bent leg.

"Get some wood," his mother said.

Isaku stood up immediately and went out through the back door. Heads of eulalia grass were swaying here and there on the rocky slope. The sun was sinking between the folds in the mountains, and the village was already half in darkness.

He picked up some firewood from the pile next to the back wall of the house.

The next morning he went fishing.

The catch would fall off at the onset of winter when the sea became rough, so before that time they would have to store as much seafood in their houses as possible. Fortunately, the autumn octopus was coming into shore in greater numbers than usual.

Out by the reef, men and boys no more than ten years old were in little boats spearing octopuses between the rocks. Isaku worked the oar of his father's boat, steering it across the water. He stopped and took hold of his long barbed fishing spear. There was a piece of red cloth attached to the tip, and he stretched it out into the water toward the shadow of rocks or near thick clumps of duckweed. When the end of the spear was jiggled slightly, the octopuses would mistake the wavering cloth for food and emerge from their hiding places in crannies in the rocks or deep in the duckweed. Isaku would then skillfully hook them with the barb of his spear.

There were so many that Isaku would sometimes find himself having to stab at as many as three or four octopuses each time he put the spear into the water.

Isaku's father had taught him how to fish and steer a boat two years earlier. Unlike his mother, Isaku's father never lifted a hand against him, but his taciturn moods struck terror into the boy. When Isaku was learning how to catch octopus, he dropped the fishing spear into the water time and time again, but his father said nothing and only glared at him as he jumped into the sea to retrieve it.

Isaku was well aware that the status of manhood hinged upon becoming an expert fisherman. Thus he was eager to learn the art, and despite his inexperience he started going out on the water with the men from the time his father left the village to go into bondage.

On the shore, the old people and young children were collecting seaweed while the women stepped into the water to pick shellfish off the rocks.

Isaku occasionally cast his eyes toward the far-off ridges as he fished for octopus. Day by day the reddish color seemed to be flowing down from the crests, tinting the surface of the mountains as it went, with the autumn hues now beginning to reach the trees on the nearer slopes.

The days became colder and the chill on the water intensified. The octopus seemed to be coming into the shore in hordes, and sometimes a simple flutter of the red cloth would lure ten of the little creatures. Isaku jerked the hook up and then waited for the cloud of ink to disappear before putting the barbed rod into the water again.

The leaves of the trees behind the village reached their full autumn splendor. As happened every year at this time, the octopus suddenly began to leave the shoreline. However much he shook the cloth on the barbed spear, only an occasional octopus would emerge, and before long they ceased to appear at all.

The octopus season came to an end, but that year's catch was better than usual. Outside each house, octopuses hung from lines of straw twine, split open to dry in the autumn sun. The octopus was not only an essential staple of New Year's but also a valuable commodity. It would be sold through the next village to people in the mountain hamlets, enabling the villagers to buy grain.

The O-fune-sama ritual was held around the time the village was enveloped in the autumn colors. With her husband at the helm, a boat carrying a twenty-eight-year-old pregnant woman moved off the thin strip of sandy beach. Looking out toward the horizon, she held up a small sacred straw festoon as the boat bobbled its way out into deeper water. It finally came to a stop after being skillfully maneuvered out past the rocks. The villagers gathered on the shore pressed their palms together in prayer when the woman tossed the festoon into the water. The pregnant woman represented their wish for a good catch of fish, and the casting of the sacred festoon into the water their hope that a passing ship would be wrecked on the reef in front of the village.

Isaku, his mother, with Teru tied to her back, his younger brother and sister, all watched the boat bob up and down as it headed back to shore. It was high tide, and the rocks were almost completely submerged, but even so the water foamed in spots.

The boat reached the shore, and the woman stepped out onto the sand. The people gathered on the beach parted ranks to let her pass, then followed behind her as she walked up the shore. Normally a cheerful woman, known for her shrieks of laughter, she seemed to be a completely different person as she walked purposefully up the slope.

Once onto the path she advanced, with slow, deliberate steps, up to the village chief's house. Isaku followed them inside, stepping onto the dirt floor of the entrance and peering between the men standing in front of him. The old village chief was sitting cross-legged, upright, a box-shaped table and a bowl full of food placed in front of him. The woman knelt, placing her hands on the floor as she bowed deeply. This was the first time Isaku had watched this ritual, because until this year he had not been permitted into the house.

The woman stood, holding up the bottom of her kimono

as she stepped toward the little table and overturned it with a solid kick. Then she knelt once more and bowed in front of the village chief. The kicking-over of the bowl expressed their desire for a ship to capsize, and with this the ceremony ended.

The villagers began to return to their homes. Work was forbidden on the day of the *O-fune-sama* ceremony, so Isaku followed his mother back along the narrow path leading to their house.

In front of them a man named Senkichi was walking with his family. He had broken his thighbone when he was small, leaving him with one leg considerably shorter than the other, but he was famous for making the best dugout boats in the village. His eldest daughter had been sold into bondage, and there was talk that his fifteen-year-old second daughter would be sold in the near future.

Isaku's eyes followed the third daughter Tami as she walked behind her father. She was dark skinned like Senkichi's wife, but she had sharp eyes and a straight nose. Her movements were lithe, like an animal's. Whenever he looked at Tami he felt strangely aroused.

In the village, when a young man turned fifteen he was allowed to make advances to the girl he wanted for his wife. It was the custom that the youth would creep into her house at night, and if the girl did not refuse him, the family would turn a blind eye to his presence. Isaku yearned for a chance to hold Tami in his arms. He worried that Tami, a year older than he was, might give herself to someone else before he reached the required age. The thought frightened him.

He was also afraid that Tami might be sold into bondage like her older sisters. Women were normally sold as maids, and few returned home after their term of bondage was over.

Some probably loathed the impoverished life in the village, and others would find a man during their indentureship and start a family once they had fulfilled their bond. Even if they did return, those who had served terms as long as ten years were too old to marry anyone except widowers. There were men with older wives, but Isaku felt that he had little hope of ever being able to live under the same roof as Tami.

They came to a fork in the path, and Tami and her parents walked off along the track parallel to the coast. Isaku stared at Tami's legs showing underneath her kimono.

A northwesterly wind began to blow.

Isaku worked hard cutting down trees in the forest, dragging them back to the house to chop into firewood. On days when the sea was calm he went out on the boat and dropped a line into the water.

The reddish color on the far ridges disappeared, and the leaves of the trees on the slope behind the village faded fast. The temperature dropped day by day. On windy days great clouds of dry leaves swirled into the air from among the rocks and fell onto the village path or the roofs of the houses. Many were blown far out to sea.

The sea became rough, and spray from the whitecaps smashing on the rocks rained onto the houses near the shore. The village was enveloped in the sound of the waves.

When the sun set, the salt-making began on the thin strip of sand by the shoreline. The women carried thirty shallow boxes from the village chief's storehouse, lined them up on the beach, filled them with sand, then poured in tubs of seawater. Once the sand dried in the sun, it was again washed with seawater. The heavily salted water would be drained into tubs and transferred to two large cauldrons placed on the shore.

Each household would supply equal amounts of firewood, and the men would take turns watching over the fires until daybreak, when the salt was ready. While this would provide an essential commodity for the villagers, the fires under the cauldrons also served to attract *O-fune-sama*.

3

Isaku lifted his bundle of dry branches onto his back and started off down the path. The sea was growing angry under the bright red sky. Whitecaps surged in, and breakers smashed onto the shore and the cape. The onset of winter was usually marked by four days of rough seas followed by two of calm; the past three days' heavy seas had made fishing impossible. Rocks were exposed everywhere along the path, and Isaku struggled to keep from toppling forward under the weight of his load.

The roofs of the houses came into view. Isaku's mother was standing beside the back door, waving at him to hurry. She seemed to have something urgent to tell him. Using a stick to keep his balance, he stepped down behind the house.

"A messenger came saying the village chief wants to see you. Get up there right away," his mother said hurriedly.

While Isaku had seen the village chief, he had never spoken to him and so had no idea why he was being summoned.

"Hurry up!" said his mother, taking his load off his back, something unheard-of for her, and giving him a good slap on the back to send him on his way. Isaku scampered off along the track. The reddish tinge to the sky was fading, and the sea was beginning to darken. The shore was wet from the waves.

He ran along the path and on up some stone steps. The old man who worked for the village chief's family was collecting grain that had been spread out on a straw mat.

Isaku entered the house and sat down, bowing deeply. The village chief was sitting beside the fireplace. Isaku introduced himself in a trembling voice, his knees shaking from the foreboding that he was about to be scolded for some offense.

"Starting tonight you're out on the salt cauldrons. It'll be your first night, so go out with Kichizo and get him to show you the ropes. After that you're on your own. Don't let the fires go out." The village chief had a thin, high-pitched voice like a child's. Isaku bowed deeply, until his forehead touched the ground.

"Off you go."

Still kneeling, Isaku shuffled back toward the entrance, stood up, and left.

His face flushed with excitement as the tension disappeared. The order to work through the night on the salt cauldrons meant that he was recognized as an adult. He had felt that this might happen ever since he had been allowed to help with the cremation, but knowing that it was actually about to come to pass filled him with irrepressible joy. He ran back along the shoreline path to his house. By now the sky was dusky gray.

He left the house carrying a flaming torch in his hand. When his mother heard that he had been ordered to watch over the fires under the cauldrons, she had become unusually cheerful and had pan-roasted beans for him to eat during the night. The torch flame flickered in the wind. He left the path and went down to the shore. He could see the color of the fire ahead of him on the beach and sensed that someone was there.

He picked up his step. The man's good eye was trained on Isaku. The other was pale and cloudy, having long since lost its glint. Isaku was indeed fortunate to have Kichizo, who was on good terms with Isaku's father, initiating him.

Large stones had been arranged in two spots on the sandy area of the beach to serve as a base for the two big cauldrons. The wood under one of them had already been lit.

"Light that one, too," said Kichizo, looking toward the second big pot about ten yards away on the beach. Isaku responded eagerly, pulling out a bundle of dried branches from under a straw mat, swinging it onto his back, and carrying it over to the other cauldron. He put the branches into the stone enclosure and lit them with a burning piece of wood. The twigs and branches crackled as they lit. Isaku placed more wood on the fire.

Flames rose from under the two cauldrons, flickering in the wind off the sea as sparks scattered on the sand. Isaku watched the flames as he sat next to Kichizo on a log inside a makeshift wooden hut.

Several years earlier, Kichizo had been afflicted with an eye disease that had left him unable to go out fishing, forcing him to sell his wife into bondage for three years. She came back to the village after she finished her term working at the port at the southern tip of the island, but as she was almost six months late returning from bondage, Kichizo suspected that she must have taken up with another man.

Whether it was true or not was unknown, but there were

rumors among the villagers that she had had a child and had extended her term in order to clean up the matter.

Kichizo had beat her violently, and in a fit of rage he even cut off her hair. On such occasions, when she had fled sobbing to Isaku's house, his father and mother had intervened. Kichizo had stopped beating his wife only after the village chief stepped in and admonished him severely. After that he had become a sullen man of few words. Often at night he used to visit Isaku's house, sometimes bringing wine made from millet. He would sit there silently, nodding as he listened to Isaku's father's fishing stories.

"You know why we make salt on the beach, don't you?" said Kichizo, his good eye trained on Isaku.

One year's supply of salt would be produced and then distributed according to the size of each family. But Isaku realized that there was another reason for Kichizo's odd question.

"It's to summon *O-fune-sama*, isn't it?" he said, looking Kichizo in the face. Kichizo said nothing, diverting his eye back to the cauldrons. From his expression, Isaku sensed that his reply had not satisfied the man.

Isaku thought that the village chief's order meant that he had to know all about tending the salt cauldrons. There was much that he didn't understand about the village rituals, but now that he was an adult he could no longer afford to remain ignorant. After this night he would have to tend the fires under the cauldrons by himself, so he needed to get Kichizo to tell him everything.

"Is it to pray for *O-fune-sama* to come in to the shore?" he asked.

"It's not just for praying. It's to attract ships passing the beach," said Kichizo impatiently.

"To attract ships?"

"That's right. When the northwest winds start to blow, the seas get rough, and more ships get in trouble. At night when the waves start to wash over the decks, they'll even throw cargo overboard to lighten the ship. At times like that, a crew will see the light from the cauldron fires and think it is from houses on the shore. Then they will turn the ships in toward the coast."

Kichizo's good eye gleamed as if he were studying Isaku. Isaku stared at Kichizo before turning to the sea. He could just make out where the starry night sky met the dark water. A vast and intricate reef lay concealed under the surface of the water. When they went out fishing, the village men would thread their little boats through the rocks, but a large vessel entering these waters would be sure to have its bottom ripped open in no time.

Isaku thought that he was finally starting to understand. He had assumed that the salt cauldrons were part of a ritual carried out in the hope that ships would be wrecked, but now he realized that it was also the means to lure ships onto the reef.

If gathering salt were the only purpose, then doing it during the daylight hours would be far more convenient, but now he understood why it was done only at night. Also, it was clear to him why the fires were not lit on calm nights; ships would have no problems navigating then.

"The fire's dying down," said Kichizo, getting to his feet.

Isaku stood up and followed Kichizo, picking up a bundle of firewood from beneath the straw mats. He went over to the cauldron on the right and threw the wood underneath.

It is said that sailors in distress during a dark, stormy night will do absolutely anything to survive. They will throw their cargo overboard, cut off their hair, and pray to the gods for protection, and if the ship seems in real danger of capsizing, they will even cut down the masts to keep it stable. To them the fires under the cauldrons on the beach could very well appear to be the lights from houses on the shore. No doubt they would think their prayers had been answered and turn their ship in toward the fires.

The wood was engulfed in flames.

When Isaku returned to the little hut, Kichizo sat down on the log and piled up dry twigs and branches on the sand. He lit them and put on some firewood. Isaku warmed his hands over the fire. The chill in the air suddenly intensified.

"These fires will bring in *O-fune-sama*, won't they?" said Isaku with a sparkle in his eyes as he looked at Kichizo.

Kichizo nodded. "Not these last few years, but when they do come, they come one after another. When I started going out fishing with your father, they came four years in a row. When I was eleven, we had three in one winter. All because of these fires. In those days no one had to sell themselves into bondage," he said in a low voice.

Isaku thought that Kichizo was so unusually talkative because he felt at ease with his friend's son. Even though he had lost the sight of one eye, if *O-fune-sama* had come, he would not have had to sell his wife into bondage and their marriage would not have been ruined.

Isaku gazed out to sea. He thought of Tami, Senkichi's third daughter. The eldest daughter had already been sold, and now there were rumors about the next daughter going into bondage. If there was no bounty from the sea in the next few years, Tami would undoubtedly follow.

Isaku became restless. If a ship had been lured onto the reef, his father would not have had to sell himself either. The lives of the villagers hinged on the coming of O-fune-sama.

"We make salt this way to ensure the fires don't go out and to get O-fune-sama to come." Kichizo's eye gleamed red with the flames from the fire.

"I wonder if it'll come this winter." Isaku looked out to sea.

"Who knows. When the wind starts to blow from the northwest, they get scared and the ships on the offshore run don't go out. But even then, when they've got cargo to carry, they choose a calm day to set sail. Mostly ships carrying rice," muttered Kichizo.

A wave of drowsiness suddenly hit Isaku as he warmed himself by the fire. His body was numb, and his eyelids started to feel heavy. If he nodded off, no doubt he would be removed from salt-making duty, and his mother would fly into a rage and beat him. The very thought of such disgrace terrified him.

Isaku stood up and ran out of the hut. A chilling wind blew off the sea. He stood on tiptoe and peered into the cauldron. Clouds of steam rose as the salt water boiled away. He checked the fire, then brought over several pieces of fire-wood, throwing them under the cauldron. In a flash his drowsiness had faded.

Dawn came.

The fires had gone out. The water had completely evaporated, leaving the sides of the cauldrons covered with a white substance almost up to the lip. At Kichizo's instruction, Isaku covered each one of them with two half-moon-shaped lids. The salt would be left to the women who would come to the shore after the cauldrons had gone cold.

His face, arms, legs, and clothes were sticky and damp from the salt air, and he felt light-headed from having worked through the night.

"Let's go," said Kichizo, starting off along the shore. Isaku followed after him up toward the path.

Steam was already floating up from the pot on the fire when he got home, and his younger brother and sister were sitting at the fireside. He hung tubs from both ends of a bucket yoke and went out to draw water from the nearby well. The sea was brighter now, and stars could be seen only faintly at one end of the sky. When he got back home, he sat beside the fire and scooped vegetable porridge into a bowl. He wanted to tell his mother about how well his work on the cauldron fires had gone, but her silence made him hesitate.

His mother scooped up some of the porridge into bowls for his brother and sister, emptying the pot. As always, she added some water to the pot. Once the water was hot Isaku poured it into his bowl and drank it. Two soggy grains of millet remained at the bottom of the bowl.

Isaku mumbled that he would like to get a little sleep. His mother remained silent. He got to his feet and slipped under his straw mat bedding. In a moment he was asleep. After a couple of hours he felt the matting being pulled off him and his cheek being slapped. Turning his head away, he raised himself on his arms.

His mother's face loomed in front of him. "You gonna sleep forever? Get up and do some work. The sea's calm." He sprang to his feet and stepped down to the dirt floor section of the house. His mother swung a basket onto her back and left the house. Shouldering his fishing tackle, Isaku followed after her. Listless from lack of sleep, he rubbed his eyes and yawned.

Down on the beach the women were scooping salt from the cauldrons and into tubs to be carried away. The salt would be taken to the village chief's house and divided up for each household.

Women, old people, and children could be seen hunched over, combing the shoreline. After several days of heavy seas they would find plenty of shellfish and seaweed washed up onto the beach. At times, pieces of wood from wrecked ships, fruit from trees in far-off places, even fragments of everyday items drifted in on the currents. His mother hurried toward the shore.

The boats were on the water. In contrast to the previous night, there was no wind; the sea was tranquil, bathed in soft sunlight. Isaku set his little boat afloat in the shallows and stepped into the cold water to push it farther out. Every time he grasped the oar he was reminded of his father. Knowing that the grip had been worn smooth by his father's palms made him feel that his father was near. He worked the oars slowly.

He could see the two iron cauldrons on the beach. One had been emptied of salt, and women gathered around the second.

Suddenly the women stopped moving and turned to look out to sea. Isaku turned his head to follow their gaze. He stopped rowing.

A ship big enough to carry three or four hundred bales of rice could be seen coming around the cape. Its sails were hanging virtually lifeless. The upper part of the sails bore two black stripes as insignia, and cargo and crew were visible on deck. The ship was slowly moving southeast.

Isaku gazed at the ship until it finally disappeared behind the small headland where the crows circled.

Not long after harvest time, ships laden with straw bales of rice became a common sight. Some plied the waters far offshore, others hugged the coastline.

Ships of the feudal clans bore a large family crest in the

middle of the sail; the ship passing the village that day had only two black stripes at the top of the sail, clearly signifying that it belonged to a merchant. It must have been waiting for the stormy weather to clear before leaving port. On days when the sea was rough the fires on the beach would be lit as soon as the sun went down.

Isaku heard that Sahei had also been ordered by the village chief to work on the salt cauldrons. It was rumored that Sahei's family had celebrated their son's coming-of-age by making buckwheat dumpling soup and drinking millet wine. Isaku was envious, but when he thought of his family's circumstances, with his father in indentured service, he realized he could hardly expect such treatment. On the contrary, he knew full well that he had to accept the fact that, with his father away, it was up to him and his mother to keep his young brother and sisters from starving.

Shifts on the salt cauldrons came every ten days. When his turn came, he would go down to the shore alone in the late afternoon and tend the fires until daybreak. If he grew drowsy, he would jump up and down around the hut or go to the water's edge and dip his feet into the cold sea, gazing out into the night and wondering whether *O-fune-sama* might be on its way.

Occasionally ships passed by during the day. Mostly when the sea was calm, but sometimes even on stormy days. Tossed about by the waves, these ships would bob up and down wildly, half-furled sails billowing in the wind as they sped away. Isaku and the other villagers stared intently at each ship as it passed. Every time he saw a vessel he realized that there would be ships passing even on stormy nights.

He heard a disturbing story from Sahei.

Sahei had appeared one morning after Isaku had finished

his third night on the cauldrons and was putting sand onto the remains of the fire in the hut.

"How's the work on the salt going?" asked Sahei as he sat down on the log in the hut.

Isaku was annoyed whenever Sahei acted as if he were the older of the two, but he did feel awed by Sahei's size and precociousness. Sahei also had a glint in his eye, the look of a worldly-wise man.

"I'm managing," said Isaku, looking away.

"Do you ever feel like nodding off?" said Sahei, studying Isaku's expression.

Isaku took this to mean that he mustn't be the only one having problems staying awake, which made him feel a little more at ease.

"I get sleepy all right." Isaku sat down on the log next to Sahei and rubbed his eyes.

"Then you're not taking it seriously enough. If you think about how important the job is, you won't be sleepy." A smirk appeared on Sahei's face. Isaku said nothing, realizing that Sahei would take advantage of the slightest chance to get an edge on him. Isaku thought that Sahei's defiant attitude might mean he was upset that Isaku had been first to receive his order from the village chief to work on the salt cauldrons.

Nevertheless, he was ready to admit that Sahei was undoubtedly right. Quite likely Sahei could get through the night without nodding off, concentrating fully on the salt cauldrons as he kept an eye on the night sea. Isaku blinked weakly, feeling small.

"You heard about O-fune-sama and the bailiff," Sahei said, looking sideways at Isaku.

Isaku turned to look at him. He had no idea what O-fune-sama could have to do with a bailiff. Isaku's father and mother seldom talked about village affairs, but in Sahei's family, his grandfather and parents discussed all manner of topics; so it was only natural that Sahei would come to learn a great deal. Sahei's knowledge was another reason Isaku felt a little intimidated by the boy.

"A bailiff?" he whispered suspiciously.

"You didn't know? You mean you started working the salt cauldrons without knowing about it?" sneered Sahei.

Isaku was irritated by Sahei's attitude, as well as somewhat uneasy. He had never seen a bailiff but certainly had heard that they were to be feared—stories of how bailiffs would arrest people, tie them up, and cut off their heads or burn them alive on a crucifix or impale them on a pike. Isaku felt crushed by Sahei's hints of a connection between O-*fune-sama* and the bailiff, and he thought his ignorance made him unfit to work the salt cauldron.

"Tell me then. What about the bailiff?" he said.

Sahei didn't reply. He was watching the women on the beach carry the salt away.

"I heard the story from my grandfather . . . ," Sahei began, explaining that it had happened when O-*fune-sama* had come one winter, sometime before his grandfather was born. That night, too, in heavy seas a ship had had its bottom smashed open on the reef after being lured to the cauldron fires lit on the shore. It was a ship of considerable size, and though the crew had jettisoned some of the cargo, there was still a large amount left.

"The people in the village were ecstatic, but they were shocked when they saw the crest on the sail," said Sahei grim-faced.

The sails had been taken down, but the large insignia on them indicated that it was a clan ship. The cargo on board

was government property, and stealing it would of course invite harsh retribution. Terror-stricken, the villagers put out
boats and rescued the captain and crew clinging to the
wrecked ship. They waited for the sea to calm before they
unloaded the cargo onto the beach and pulled the sails and
the smashed pieces of ship's timber up onto the shore. Also,
they retrieved the bodies of two drowned clansmen, one crew-
man, and a galley boy who had been washed overboard and
found at the foot of the cape.

A messenger was sent to the next village over the ridge,
and seven days later a young bailiff appeared, accompanied
by two attendants. The village chief and the other people
in the village prostrated themselves on the ground in the
chief's courtyard to greet the bailiff.

The villagers were afraid that the bailiff would suspect
that the fires under the salt cauldrons were for luring passing
ships onto the rocks. Trembling with fear, the chief had kept
his forehead to the ground, muttering simple replies to the
bailiff's questions.

Fortunately the official did not catch on to the villagers'
secret. He thought it only natural that they would be making
salt on the beach and saw nothing strange in the fact that
the sailors might mistake the fires for houses and turn their
ship toward the treacherous rocks lining the coast. On the
contrary, upon hearing the testimony of the rescued sailors,
the bailiff was pleased at how the villagers had handled the
clan ship. Everyone in the village helped to lay the cargo and
broken pieces of wood from the ship out to dry in the sun,
or piled them inside the village chief's house or in the yard.
Also, the four bodies that had been recovered were temporarily interred in one corner of the yard, and a black flag of
mourning was put up.

The bailiff seemed to think that the villagers were blame-less, and left with the ship's survivors. In due course, he ap-peared in the village again, this time with some men leading several oxen. They collected the ship's cargo that had been stored at the village chief's house, lashed it onto the oxen, and carried it away. They took the sailcloth but let the vil-lagers keep what was left of the wrecked ship.

Though the village benefited very little, the people were greatly relieved to have avoided punishment. But their fears were not easily allayed, and no more salt was made that year. They regained their composure with the first signs of spring. Soon, however, they were gray with fear again as they were tormented by another unexpected calamity.

One day, three men leading some oxen appeared on the mountain path. One of these unsavory-looking characters, wearing a sword in a faded scabbard, presented himself at the village chief's house.

Claiming to be a bailiff, he shouted angrily that people in the village were hiding cargo from the wrecked clan ship. Petrified, the village chief pleaded with him in a trembling voice. But the men paid no heed, and the next day they made everyone in the village, including the village chief, empty their larders of stored provisions and lash everything onto the pack animals, menacing the people with their swords as they drove the oxen back up the mountain path.

After they had left, the villagers realized that these men had merely been posing as bailiffs, and they prepared hatchets and gaffs, resolving to kill the impostors should they return. But they were never to be seen again.

"The daimyo's ships are big and sail out in deep water, so they run far off the coast. They're sturdily built, so not many get wrecked. O-fune-sama are the ones on the coastal run, merchant ships passing close by. But as I said, even the daimyo's ships can end up as *O-fune-sama*. Both my grand-father and my father have told me, if *O-fune-sama* comes when you are looking after the fires, the first thing you have to do is take a look at the crest on the sails. Didn't anyone tell you that?" Sahei said.

Isaku shook his head. He was annoyed that Kichizo hadn't seen fit to mention the sails in his instructions. He felt sure that in the same way as Sahei had heard from his grandfather and father, he, too, would have been warned to look out for the insignia on the sails, had his father been at home.

"Is there anything else I should know?" asked Isaku, gen-uinely grateful that Sahei had told him about the marks on the sails.

Sahei pensively tilted his head to one side as he looked across the beach and then, almost as an afterthought, said, "My father told me that if you do see *O-fune-sama*, you should run straight to the village chief's house and tell him. Don't run home or anything like that." Isaku thought that this, too, was something he should bear in mind. He could certainly imagine how the shock of seeing *O-fune-sama* might make him run home to tell his mother.

On the beach the women were working hard scooping salt from the cauldrons and putting it into wooden tubs. Clouds raced across the sky, and spray from the waves splashed on the shore.

"It seems my dad might be going into bondage, too," Sahei murmured as he gazed out to sea.

Sahei had a sister who was already married, another older sister aged fourteen, and a brother two years younger than Sahei. By all accounts Sahei's family had celebrated the night he had been instructed to work on the cauldrons, but perhaps they were just as short of food as Isaku's family after all. The fourteen-year-old daughter was next in line to be sold into bondage, but if she came back after finishing her service, she would be too old to marry by then. Most likely Sahei's father had made his decision to sell himself out of pity for his daughter.

"My grandfather's home crying. He says he'd sell himself if he were a little younger." Sahei tried to force the sullen look from his face.

If *O-fune-sama* were to come, there would be no need for Sahei's father to sell himself. No doubt Sahei was putting his all into the work on the cauldrons, wishing with all his heart that *O-fune-sama* would come so his father would not have to leave the village.

Drowsiness started to get the better of Isaku. He stood up. "I'm going to get some sleep," he said to Sahei, still sitting on the log. He picked up the dead pine torch and headed toward his house.

The next morning saw the first flurry of snow. Nothing more than a few flakes, barely perceptible on the blustery winds, but it grew heavier in the afternoon, whirling into the house past the fluttering straw mat hanging at the entrance.

Isaku was working hard chopping firewood on the dirt floor while his mother mended the children's tattered clothes. The cloth was made of thread woven from the inner fibers of the bark from young linden trees growing in the mountains, but none had been collected this summer.

Every year in early summer his father would go into the mountains to get linden saplings. With his father away this year Isaku had his hands full, but he resolved to go into the woods to collect bark from the saplings next summer.

His brother and sisters were sitting huddled together beside the fire. There was still the grain they had bought with Isaku's father's bondage payment, but with no other food to be had through the winter, they would have to ration their supplies sparingly until spring. His father's parting words, "Don't let the children starve," uttered so gravely before he went into bondage, weighed heavily on Isaku's heart.

The snow continued to fall throughout the next day, then stopped the following morning, leaving the village covered in a blanket of white.

Isaku and the men put their boats onto the water while his mother went down to comb the shoreline. He hung a line over the side but could only catch the smallest of fish, and very few at that. The currents would have taken the schools of fish far offshore, and the octopus and squid must have been driven by the crashing waves to the seaward side of the reef to find a place to rest.

When the sea was calm, and occasionally even on stormy days, they would see ships passing with their sails half-furled. Among these were ships bearing large insignia in the middle of their sails.

The old year came to a close and a new year began. The villagers observed the five-day New Year's holiday. They stayed inside, lighting fires every morning and night in front of their houses to drive away demons. Laughter was forbidden because it was thought to bring back luck, and even speaking was frowned upon.

On the sixth day of the year the taboo was lifted, but a gloomy atmosphere clung to the village. The shipping of rice had all but come to an end, and only a few ships would be seen passing on calm days, with none risking its sail in stormy weather. There seemed to be little hope of O-fune-sama's coming that winter, so the villagers could do nothing but wait for the arrival of spring. Nevertheless, on stormy nights they continued to light the fires under the salt cauldrons. They had already produced more than enough to supply the needs of the village for the next year, but the surplus would be stored, to be sold in spring in the village over the ridge, and the money earned would be used to buy grain or fishing implements.

It was agony tending the salt cauldrons on snowy nights. Again and again Isaku would carry firewood through the driving snow and throw it under the cauldrons. The snow appeared to dance wildly, glimmering red from the color of the flames. Once into February, they were hit by a blizzard. The houses were snowed in; it was almost dark inside. Isaku and his mother cleared the snow from the roof and outside the windows, making a space for the sunlight to shine in.

In the middle of that month Teru fell ill with a high fever. Isaku's mother boiled some water, filling the room with steam, and brewed an infusion of medicinal herbs. But his little sister was not even swallowing, so his mother forced it down Teru's throat mouth-to-mouth.

At dawn the next morning Teru's body was cold. His mother's eyes were filled with tears as she quietly caressed Teru's little face.

Several men and women from neighboring houses gathered, walking behind Isaku's mother as she carried Teru's body wrapped in straw matting up the mountain path toward the graveyard. When the fire was lit in the crematory, Isaku's mother squatted beside it, struggling to keep herself from sobbing openly. Isaku looked out to sea, tears streaming down his face. His father had entrusted him and his mother with the lives of his younger brother and sisters, and now he anguished because they had not been able to keep their promise. He imagined that his mother was thinking about his father.

The horizon appeared faintly white in the distance. Isaku sensed that winter, too, was coming to an end.

4

The men who set rabbit traps in the
woods returned to the village saying they had seen blossom
on *ume* trees in a valley.

The only way the villagers could see flowers was to go
into the mountains; the salt winds that lashed the village
prevented any flowering plants or trees from surviving on the
coast. The next morning the village chief instructed them to
guide one of the village elders to the valley. When their find-
ing had been confirmed, the chief ordered salt production
stopped. The blooming of plum trees signified the end of winter and their hopes of *O-fune-sama*'s appearing. The men suspended the cauldrons from poles and carried them from the
beach to the village chief's house, where they were washed
with fresh water and coated with fish oil before being stored
away.

The village was shrouded in gloom. When the villagers
passed each other on the path, they said little, often merely
nodding a tentative greeting.

The temperature rose and the snow covering the village began to melt. At times the sound of avalanches could be heard from the mountains. Plumes of snow dust rose from the deeply chiseled valleys. Days of rough seas became infrequent, and occasionally mist would rise off the calm sea. It was said that peach trees were starting to bloom in the mountains.

The village chief ordered some men and women to sell salt in the next village. Isaku's mother was one of those chosen. Carrying straw bales full of salt on their shoulders and steadying themselves with sticks, they trudged slowly in line up the path through patches of snow toward the pass. Six days later they returned with bales of grain tied to their backs. This was divided among the households according to the number of mouths there were to feed.

In early March, Isaku joined the other villagers on the beach to pray for a good catch of fish that year. In one of the small boats they set up a sacred straw festoon suspended from a four-handed scoop net made of cotton between two thin bamboo rods.

When the village chief arrived at the beach in ceremonial attire, the boat was pushed into the water and its owner took up the oar while his pregnant wife stepped in to join him. The boat pulled away from the shore, bamboo rods swaying each time the man worked the oar, the scoop net fluttering slightly in the breeze. About forty yards offshore the boat stopped.

Facing out to sea, the woman got to her feet, and almost in a fanning motion she vigorously pulled up the bottom of her kimono. By displaying her swollen belly and her vagina to the Sea God, she was praying for the fish to breed prolifically. Isaku and the other people on the beach held their palms together in prayer. Each time she rolled up her kimono she exposed her stocky thighs and buttocks. The woman's movements continued until the man, holding the oar in one hand, poured wine from a jar into the sea with his free hand. At this, the woman released her kimono and sat down. Then her husband rowed back to the shore. On the beach she followed the village chief up to his house, where she was served a ceremonial meal.

From that day on, except when the sea was rough, Isaku joined the other fishermen on the water. As was usual around this time, large sardines started appearing. Day by day they increased in number, and no sooner would a line be in the water than a fish would be hooked. There were plenty of good-sized, choice fish among these schools, and they put up a good fight on the line. They could either be eaten raw or ground into a paste to make dumplings to put into soup. Or sometimes Isaku's mother would split them in half and hang them out to dry, saving their insides in a tub to use as fertilizer for the fields.

When the sardine catch began to slacken, five people left the village in the rain to sell themselves into indentured service. Among them were Sahei's father and Tami's sixteen-year-old elder sister. They were accompanied to the next village by family members who would receive the payment from the broker. The line of sedge hats made its way up the winding mountain path and came to a halt halfway. They seemed to be agonizing over leaving their birthplace, knowing that some people died in servitude and that even if they survived, they would not see their village again until their term was over. The line of sedge hats moved off again, swaying as it proceeded until it melted away into the gray murk of the rain.

After the sardines, squid began to appear. Isaku happened to see Sahei awkwardly hauling squid into his boat. Sahei's father had indentured himself for five years, but it was rumored that he had brought in only fifty silver *momme*, less than Isaku's father had received for a three-year term. Most villagers agreed that this was a fair price, considering Sahei's father's sloping shoulders and slight build. With his father gone, the burden of looking after the family now rested on Sahei.

There was a tormented look on Sahei's face as he worked his fishing line; his disconsolate eyes turned in Isaku's direction.

Isaku caught sight of Tami combing the store for shellfish and seaweed with the other women and children. Tami's elder sister had been sold into bondage for seven years; when she finished her service, her only prospects for marriage would be widowers. Tami was of large build, and if she were to lie about her age, the go-between would surely find someone who would take her. If Tami were sold into bondage, Isaku wanted to wait for her to return to the village after her term was up and marry her. But a wife was essential to a household; there was no way he would be able to stay single until then.

Isaku engrossed himself in catching squid. They would not be eaten right away but would be split open and dried. There were squid hanging everywhere—on ropes, under the eaves of the houses, in nearby open spaces. From the water the village looked like a hive of activity.

One evening in early April, Isaku came home, fishing tackle in hand, to find his cousin Takichi sitting with his back against the wall, arms wrapped around his knees. Isaku's mother was tying up dried squid into bundles with twine, but as soon as she saw her son she stood up, attached a bamboo basket to each end of a carrying rod, and left the house. Isaku did the same, following his mother to the shore with a carrying rod and baskets on his shoulders. They scooped the squid out of the bottom of the boat and put them into the baskets, which they then hooked onto the carrying rods.

"Takichi's getting married tomorrow, so he's staying with us tonight," his mother said as she walked back to the house.

So Kura and Takichi are finally tying the knot, Isaku thought. They were both seventeen. Kura was the most sturdily built girl in the village, and tall as well. She wore extra-large straw sandals and often did heavy work with the men. By contrast, Takichi was puny. He might have been born a fisherman, but physically he was quite frail. With his long, slender face and pigeon-toed gait there was little about him that was masculine.

Isaku had often heard the rumor that they first knew each other out in the woods, meeting by chance while collecting firewood. By all accounts, it was Takichi who was seduced. But such outdoor encounters were frowned upon, so Takichi had complied with Kura's family's request and started to visit her regularly at night.

Quite some time had passed since Takichi's father and older brother had been swept out to sea while fishing, and he now lived with his mother. She spent most of her time lying down, complaining about the pain in her hunched back. Rumor had it that Takichi's mother was very eager to see her son marry such a sturdy young woman as Kura and relentlessly urged him to the girl's house.

On the night before the wedding the man had to stay away from his own house, and on the wedding day the young girls among his relatives would accompany the go-between to the bride's house to take part in her farewell dinner, and then lead the bride and her parents to the bridegroom's house. There, the bride, fully adorned for the occasion, would exchange nuptial cups with her mother-in-law, after which the celebration would begin, and the mother-in-law would serve the bride a heaped wooden bowl of rice. While this was happening, the man would stay in hiding, coming back to the house late at night to consummate the marriage.

Isaku's house had been chosen because Takichi would feel at ease staying with relatives.

Isaku and his mother carried the squid into the house. His mother's expression suggested she was pleased with the size of the day's catch. Takichi stood up by the wall and asked, "Is there anything I can do to help?"

"A man about to get married doesn't have to lift a finger. You just sit back and think about your bride's tail." Visibly relieved, Takichi sat down again.

Steam started to rise from the vegetable porridge in the pot over the fire, and Takichi joined Isaku and his family around the fireplace. There had been a chill in the home since his father had gone into bondage, but somehow Takichi's presence seemed to improve things. Isaku's younger brother and sister cast contented looks in their guest's direction. Occasionally, as though he were remembering something, the hint of a smile would appear on Takichi's face as he ate. After the meal Isaku's mother picked up a knife and started gutting the squid on the dirt floor.

Isaku sat opposite his cousin and next to the fireplace. He wanted to ask how Takichi had courted Kura and how he had made love to her, but held back for fear of his mother's ire.

Isaku asked Takichi about saury fishing, which was due to start soon. During the rainy season the previous year, Isaku had gone after these fish but caught nothing, even though the waters were supposedly teeming with them. Takichi, on the other hand, had already proven himself as a fisherman, and Isaku envied the way his cousin was able to provide for his aged mother.

"Once you get the knack you can catch them blind-folded," said Takichi softly.

"I just can't get it. But I've got to try and catch as many as I can to keep my brother and sister from starving."

Takichi stared at his obviously distraught cousin and said, "When we start fishing, bring your boat over beside mine and I'll show you how."

"Please!" said Isaku imploringly.

The fishy smell of squid innards began to hang heavy in the air.

The following evening Isaku's mother went out to join her relatives in Takichi's house while Isaku stayed home, gutting the squid in her place. She came back after dark, her face red and puffy from wine.

"It must be about time you went and got busy with your wife," she said to Takichi, who was sitting near the fireplace. He nodded, thanked his aunt for letting him stay the night, and took his leave. Isaku's mother sat down on the straw matting.

Isaku was sitting beside the fireplace, and when he happened to look at his mother's face, glowing for an instant in the firelight, he was frightened by the strange look in her eyes. They were glazed and misty with tears. He assumed she was thinking about his father and his dead baby sister.

When parties of villagers went to the neighboring town to sell dried fish or salt, they would always call on the labor contractor's. This was the only way they could hear news of their indentured kin. Sometimes they would hear reports of deaths, or that the person was ailing. Without exception,

those who were sick would eventually die, but even knowing
this, the family would pray for their loved one's recovery.
There was no news of Isaku's father, which meant that he
was almost certainly free from illness and working safely
somewhere.

Isaku moved away from the fireplace and curled up under
his straw matting, his eyes barely open as he peered at his
mother's face.

The mountains turned a deep shade of green. Light winds,
seldom stronger than a breeze, started coming in mostly from
the east. Flies began to exhibit their prolific powers of breed-
ing and swarmed over the squid hanging out to dry. When
evening came, buzzing mosquitoes flitted by one's ear.

Occasionally cargo vessels would pass by, but the villagers
barely looked up from the job at hand as the ships retreated
steadily into the distance across the calm sea.

The number of squid caught began to dwindle, and fewer
were seen hanging out to dry. Those already dried were tied
up with twine and packed away.

On early mornings in mid-May people carrying bundles
of dried squid on their backs would appeared on the path, to
be joined by others as they climbed up the mountain path.

His mother, too, twice carried such bundles of squid to
the next village. The amount of grain she brought back in
return was nothing to speak of, but she seemed cheerful all
the same. She had stopped in at the labor contractor's to ask
about his father, and there was no news. No news was good
news; he must still be fit and well. Isaku felt relieved at this,
but then he heard his mother say that Tami's elder sister had
fallen sick after working only two months.

"And the broker's got the gall to complain that he's been

had—after he's been paid a big fat commission," his mother said, spitting out the words in outrage.

If a bond servant died, the broker would have to pay a certain amount of compensation to the employer on the grounds that he had provided an unfit worker. For this reason the broker would choose only physically sound people. To cover a possible financial loss from a worker's death, he would pay the bond servant's family a great deal less than what he got from the employer. Isaku's village provided a good supply of workers.

No doubt Tami's family would have heard by now, but Isaku wondered how they might take the news. Of course they would be distraught; but he thought they might harbor other thoughts as well. They had already received the bond payment, and Tami's sister's departure meant they had one less mouth to feed. On top of that, even if she were able to return to the village after finishing her bond service, in terms of age she would be unable to command a favorable match. In this respect, the news that Tami's sister had fallen sick with what could only be a fatal illness might not necessarily be viewed as misfortune for the family.

Putting the grain she had brought back into an urn in the larder, his mother muttered, "There's no way your father's dead. He's too strong," almost as though she were trying to admonish herself for a moment's doubt.

In the evening of the day after his mother returned from her second trip taking dried squid to the next village, Isaku was pulling his boat onto the shore when he heard the man beside him say, "There's a rainbow," as he removed the oar from his boat. Looking up, he could see it stretching faintly from the top of the mountain ridges to the sea. The first rainbow of the year.

"The saury'll be here soon," said the man enthusiastically as he swung his oar onto his shoulder and headed up the shore.

The colors of the rainbow gradually deepened, emblazoning the evening sky. Rainbows in the late afternoon were seen as a good omen, especially those in early summer, which were judged to herald a good saury season. But Isaku felt uneasy as he watched the rainbow. His skill at catching saury left much to be desired, and if his haul was as poor as the previous year's, his family would go hungry. The saury season was crucial for the villages, as the very survival of their families through that year hinged on their ability to stock up on this vital source of nourishment. Takichi had said he would teach Isaku the knack of catching saury, but maybe that had merely been a lighthearted slip of the tongue the day before his wedding.

Isaku occasionally saw Takichi on the shore, and sometimes caught sight of him fishing way out on the water. Whether or not it was because he had claimed a wife was not clear, but Takichi seemed to have a hint of self-confidence in his eyes. Though Takichi was small, Isaku felt that he looked down on him with an air of condescension. Isaku imagined that Takichi's demeanor meant that his cousin would not teach him how to catch saury after all.

But an even more dramatic change in Kura caught the attention of the villagers. She would come down to the shore as soon as she saw that Takichi had returned from the day's fishing. She was a different person in Takichi's presence, meekly following his every instruction. Strong as she was, she would effortlessly swing the large tub holding the day's catch onto her shoulder and hurry back to their house. Takichi would saunter up the slope virtually empty-handed. Smiling lasciviously, the villagers would joke that Takichi must have knocked the stuffing out of her.

On days when the sea was rough, Isaku would tie a hatchet and twine to a carrying frame and go into the woods to collect bark from linden trees for making cloth. Snakes were common among the thicker groves of linden trees, so Isaku wore leggings on top of close-fitting trousers.

It was raining only lightly, but the wind was strong. Isaku held down the edge of his sedge hat to keep it from being blown off as he made his way up the damp mountain path.

After walking for about an hour he stepped into the forest. The treetops were swaying wildly, but there was no wind inside the grove and the dank smell of bark hung in the air. He stopped beside a young linden tree and untied the hatchet and twine from his back frame. His father had taken him collecting linden bark twice in the past, and just like his father, Isaku sank the hatchet blade low into the tree, down near the roots. He cut a branch off the next tree, fashioned it into the shape of a spatula, and inserted the point under the bark, which lifted enough for him to grab and pull. The bark peeled away up the trunk.

He moved from one young tree to another, stripping away bark as he went. Drops of rain fell noisily onto his hat. The water streaming down the trunks of the linden trees glistened.

His stomach told him it was time to eat. He opened a little package of bamboo sheath and dug into the large millet dumpling wrapped inside. Last year he hadn't collected any linden bark, but this year he would be able to get his mother to make some cloth for them. As he stared at the bark he had peeled from the trees, he felt that he had become the grown-up head of the family.

He worked for a little while longer before finally collecting all the peeled bark, folding it in half, tying it up with twine, and lashing it onto the carrying frame which he then swung onto his back. It was heavy, around sixty or seventy pounds.

Using his stick for support, Isaku cautiously threaded his way through the trees and out of the forest. The rain had grown heavier, throwing up spray as it pelted his hat and shoulders. The wind bore down on his load, and he felt his body moving with it. Isaku walked on down the path, stopping occasionally to steady himself against the gusts of wind. The stormy sea came into view below him. He was soaked to the skin with rain and sweat.

His mother started preparing the bark that night. She trimmed off the outer part with a knife and laid out the inner layers on the floor. Isaku repaired his fishing tackle on the dirt floor as he watched his mother, who seemed to relish her task.

The next day she soaked the inner layers of bark in the stream near their house. The pieces of outer bark were bundled up in a corner, ready to be used as kindling. Five days later she pulled the bark out of the stream and boiled it in a potful of water mixed with ash. Then she soaked it in the stream once again, rinsed it thoroughly, and hung it up to dry in the shade before pulling it apart to make into thread. His mother spun the thread on the spinning wheel and then sat in front of the loom, weaving it into cloth. It was tiring work; occasionally she stopped to rub the sleep from her eyes.

The wet season started and sheets of rain fell on the village. The villagers had seen the last of the squid, and now they caught nothing but small fry.

In the evening an old fisherman came back to the shore to report that the saury were starting to come in.

Isaku felt himself losing his composure. His father was gifted at catching saury, but for Isaku it was a trick he could not master for the life of him. The previous rainy season he had tried to fish as he remembered his father doing, but had caught nothing at all. Isaku's family had to stand by helplessly as the smoke from other houses grilling saury floated up day after day, and everywhere people could be seen packing salted saury into barrels. This year, he thought, he had to catch some fish, even if it wasn't a lot, for his family.

Since the saury season provided the most important catch of the year for the village, the men tried their best to catch as much as they could; they had no leeway for teaching fishing techniques to others. The previous season, the other villagers had taken pity on Isaku's family and had each brought them a few fish, but this year he didn't want to depend on such charity.

The only person Isaku could rely on was his cousin Takichi, but now that he had his own household to look after, it was doubtful that he would teach Isaku how to fish. Besides, Isaku was concerned that Takichi had changed since getting married. But Isaku knew there was no way he could let his family starve, so that same evening, after hastily eating his dinner, he hurried along the moonlit path to his cousin's house.

"Hello?" Isaku said as he poked his head through the straw matting hanging at the entrance. Takichi looked toward the door from where he sat on the earthen floor, his wife kneeling beside him. There were several pieces of thick straw matting laid out on the floor, as well as some stout lengths of rope. Seeing that Takichi was starting to prepare his fishing tackle, Isaku walked toward him.

"You said you'd tell me how to catch saury. I want you to teach me. My family's gonna starve. I hope you haven't forgotten what you said that night," Isaku said.

"I haven't forgotten. I thought you'd turn up before long," Takichi said. A faint smile appeared on his face.

Isaku felt relieved. He sat down beside his cousin and turned his gaze toward Takichi's busy hands.

When fishing for saury, a fisherman would tie together three or four pieces of thick straw matting and attach a heavy rope to it, letting this drift up to about forty yards out behind the stern of the boat. At the same time, over the gunwale, he would float a piece of straw matting with seaweed hanging underneath. After dropping the anchor, he would lie flat so as not to be seen by the fish. Eventually, when he sensed that a school of saury had come under the matting, he would gently pull the matting closer with the rope. The fish would move with it and also swim under the matting attached to the gunwale. The seaweed hanging down and the floating matting would excite the saury, and they would suddenly start to lay eggs. The fisherman would put his hand through one of the several holes in the matting and move his fingers in the water. Attracted by this, the saury would slip in between the man's fingers and be caught in an instant.

While Isaku knew the basics of the procedure, he had never managed to catch anything. He had come as close as getting the fish between his fingers, but then they would get away. Also, the saury seemed to shun his boat, unlike the others.

The straw matting that would trail from the stern of the boat lay on the floor, finished, and Takichi was now making the holes in the matting that would be hung over the side of the boat.

"When I was at your house, I said you could bring your boat up alongside mine and watch from there, but come to think of it, I can't let you do that. It'd scare the fish away. Ask me anything you like, and I'll tell you, though," Takichi said as he worked on the matting.

Isaku had thought this might happen. Once the saury season started, the men became overly sensitive and would yell at other fishermen if they brought their boats within a certain distance. A keen second sight was necessary with saury fishing, and the slightest distraction could ruin a day's catch, so there was nothing strange about Takichi's refusing to let Isaku bring his boat in too close.

"Tell me how to grab the fish. They always get away from me," Isaku said, looking up at Takichi's face. Takichi stopped what he was doing and lifted one hand, moving his fingers slowly in the air before suddenly clenching them together.

"You grab the fish when you feel its head between your fingers. They get away because you grab too low."

"The head," said Isaku, moving his own fingers in the air.

"If you let one get through your fingers, they won't come back again. And when you go to grab them, make sure you don't dig your fingers in. They'll scatter if they smell their blood in the water." Isaku nodded as Takichi started working again.

"One more thing. Why is it the fish don't come near my boat?"

Takichi looked up as he replied. "They can see your shadow on the water. Lie down flat inside the boat and just poke your arm over the side. Saury get scared when they sense someone there."

Isaku knew all this, but he obviously wasn't being careful enough.

Takichi looked down at the straw matting. Isaku stared at him, impressed that his cousin was a full-fledged fisherman at the age of seventeen. Clearly, looking after his mother and now being a husband to Kura had imbued him with a strong sense of responsibility. Isaku could not help but see his cousin in a new light.

Anxious to get home to start putting together his fishing gear, Isaku thanked Takichi and Kura and left. He started working that night and resumed early the next morning. It was almost midday by the time he finished.

Isaku and his mother carried the gear down to the beach through the light rain and loaded it into his boat. Dusk was said to be the best time for fishing, so there were no boats out on the water yet.

He went down to the shore again after lunch to find the men getting ready to put their boats out. The saury would come in from the west; the men would fish around the tip of the headland protruding out on the left, about two and a half miles from the beach. Boats were leaving the shore one after another, so Isaku, too, put his headband on and pushed his boat into the water. Grasping the oar he worked his way out through the reef. The sea was so calm that the waves barely lapped onto the cape. The rows of houses in the village faded into the distance as the expanse of mountains unfolded behind them. The rain had stopped, but clouds of mist clung to the wooded slopes.

Isaku worked the oar with all his strength, but one by one the other boats overtook him. Sahei's was the only one he could see behind him.

His boat started to pitch and roll as he approached the

cape and the open sea behind it. The men ahead of him had already started fishing by the time Isaku pulled in his oar, dropped anchor, and let the straw matting out into the water over the stern. The mats bobbed up and down with the swell of the sea as they drifted farther out, pulling the rope tight. Isaku put the last piece just over the side of the boat, recalling Takichi's advice as he pressed his body flat and looked out astern toward the floating pieces of matting. According to Takichi, he should slowly pull on the rope to bring the matting in toward the boat once he sensed that a school of saury were underneath, but he could see no sign of any fish. Other men were already hauling in the ropes as they lay flat in their boats.

He kept a close watch on his matting but saw no noticeable change. Yet, he thought, there may be a school of saury under there after all. He grabbed the rope and started to pull. The matting came slowly in toward the boat. It was heavy.

When the matting reached the boat, he tied the rope to the stern. Isaku reached out toward the matting floating from the gunwale, put his hand through one of the holes, opened his fingers, and slowly moved them in the water. He focused on the area under the matting. He could see silvery, shining flashes darting by. They're here all right, he thought.

The silver-colored shining things gradually increased in number and began to seethe below the surface. Some even seemed to stop for an instant. Saury brushed against his fingers and then were gone. He remembered Takichi's advice that if he missed the first fish, the whole school would scatter. Saury started to flit through his fingers. He could clearly see the heads. Several times he thought, *Grab it!* but his fingers did not move.

When he saw a saury's head passing between his fingers,

he clutched at it hastily, but the fish did a shimmy and slipped away. The school of saury seemed to disappear in a flash, as did the silvery luminescence.

Isaku took his hand out of the water and rubbed his face roughly. Once again he had been reminded that fishing for saury was not going to be an easy job and that catching them by hand would not be something mastered quickly. He tried to console himself, thinking that he hadn't done so badly after all, that the previous year he had hardly ever managed to get the fish to come under the matting, let alone have them swarm around his fingers.

Around him he could see men grabbing fish and dropping them in the bottom of their boats. Light rain started to fall. Isaku let out the rope and the straw matting once more, waited what he judged to be the right length of time, then hauled it back in, but there was no sign of any saury under the matting.

A short while later the sea began to turn a dark murky color, and the men began to turn their boats back to shore. Isaku pulled up the matting, grasped his oar, and followed behind them. Threading his way through the reef behind the boat in front of him, he worked his way to the fire lit on the beach. Night was settling in and the people standing on the beach appeared red in the firelight.

Isaku guided his boat up onto the beach, then pulled it farther up the shore with his mother. She said nothing as she ran her eyes over the bottom of the boat.

That night he went to see Takichi again. The smell of grilled saury and smoke from the cooking fire still hung in the air in Takichi's house.

"Not even one," sighed Isaku as he sat himself down on the edge of the bed, but Takichi merely smiled faintly from beside the fireplace.

"How do you know when the fish have come under the matting out behind the boat?" asked Isaku.

"Instinct, experience. . . . Water changes color slightly. Seems to move, too," replied Takichi.

Isaku said nothing. His cousin stood up, saying, "Eat this," holding out some grilled saury on skewers. Isaku shook his head frantically, got to his feet, and left the house without saying a word.

Except on days when the sea was rough, Isaku put his boat out every day with the other fishermen. The saury season was approaching its peak, and the catch increased day by day. It seemed that Sahei had been taught by his father, too, and almost without fail he brought back ten fish a day. The other men came back with the bottoms of their boats covered with saury.

Isaku felt ashamed to be heading back to shore without having caught anything at all. His mother said nothing about his fishing and made a thin vegetable and rice porridge for his younger brother and sister. The fact that he couldn't catch any fish for them tormented Isaku.

About two weeks after he'd started going out after saury, Isaku noticed a faint hint of spray in the water near the straw matting. Not only that, he felt he could just make out a difference in the color of the water at that spot. Maybe his eyes were playing a trick on him, he thought. The sea was calm, with only the slightest of swells and no suggestions of any change. He thought there was no way he would ever be able to judge whether or not fish were there.

Isaku grasped the rope and gently started to reel it in. He thought, There's nothing to lose if there's no saury there. The matting came closer, finally lining up alongside that tied to the gunwale. Tying up the rope, he sneaked a look under the matting.

He could see a seething mass of shiny, silver-colored objects. Isaku felt flushed with excitement. His eyes hadn't been deceiving him after all. He had actually been able to detect the fish's presence from a distance of forty yards. No doubt it was simple for the other fishermen, but for Isaku this was very much a milestone.

Stretching out his hand, he slowly dipped it into the sea between the mats and began to move his outspread fingers flauntingly. The water under the matting was teeming with saury. These fish were in prime condition, beautiful both in terms of shape and color. Their little eyes gleamed. The fish started to pass through his fingers. He saw one of them pause right in his hand. Lifting his hand out of the water, he looked at the struggling saury, its body glistening in the afternoon sun. Tears came to his eyes. He was elated at the thought that he would be able to feed the fish to his little brother and sister sipping on their thin rice soup by the fireside.

Isaku placed the fish in the bottom of the boat and put his arm into the water again through a hole in the matting.

That night his mother cut the saury into four equal portions, skewered each one, and held them up over the fire. A hint of smoke rose, and the flames flared a little each time some oil dripped into the fire from the skewered saury. His brother and sister stared at the fish, their eyes glowing.

His mother handed him the skewered head portion and gave the other three to his brother and sister. Isaku realized that serving him the head was his mother's way of acknowledging him as the breadwinner of the family.

The hot saury was delicious. The sight of his brother and sister wolfing down the flesh of the fish and then sucking on the bones made him realize that he would have to keep bringing more.

That season turned out to be exceptional. As the days went by, more and more saury seemed to swarm under the matting. In the short time they were on the water, the fishermen were grabbing one saury after another, and the majority of the boats were returning to shore loaded with more than a hundred fish.

Eventually Isaku, too, seemed to learn the technique involved, and before long he was catching several saury a day. Occasionally there were even days when he would bring back as many as ten. His mother rationed them to one fish a day and preserved the others in salt.

One night the rainy season came to a crescendo with peals of thunder and a furious downpour. After that the sun became stronger, and with it Isaku's arms and legs turned a dark shade of brown. The women were hard at work collecting seaweed. The summer heat intensified, and at times the village was drenched by showers. The saury began moving north, growing scarcer by the day, until suddenly in early July they vanished altogether. Squid started to appear again, and the men worked hard to hook them using pieces of little fish as bait.

The women of the village carried salted saury on their backs to the next town. They had caught enough to store for their own needs and wanted to trade the surplus for grain. But this year all the coastal villages had experienced similarly large catches, and more than half the fish were being used as fertilizer for the fields, so they came back with very little grain to show for their efforts. Of course Isaku's family had been able to store away only a small amount of salted saury, so they had not gone to the next village.

Those who made the trip came back telling of how a fever had killed many people in other villages that summer. But thanks to its isolation, no one in Isaku's village had suffered from this sickness. Other than the very young, most who had perished had been either old people or those whose brain or lungs had been fatally damaged by the disease.

Worried about the risk of a contagious disease being brought in from outside, the village chief prohibited anyone from leaving the village. He ordered those who had returned from the next village to wash themselves in the sea, without fail, early each morning for two weeks.

The time of the Bon festival came, and the fishing season was brought to a halt.

Family groups of villagers headed up the mountain path to clean the graves of their ancestors before returning to their houses to place offerings of grain or dried fish on their own Buddhist altars. In the evening they would burn a hemp stalk at their doorway, and flaming torches would be driven into the sandy part of the beach. It was said that the souls who had departed for a distant place across the ocean would rely on these torches to find their way back through the darkness as far as the beach; the light of the burning hemp stalks would guide them home. They believed that the spirits would wash their feet before entering the house, so the villagers prepared a washtub full of fresh water and placed it in the entrance.

For Isaku's mother this would be the first Bon since Teru had died in February of that year, so she tied a piece of white cloth to a thin bamboo rod she had cut herself, and stood this at the door. The pain of losing a child seemed to come back to her again as she stood there beside the bamboo rod for quite some time.

Three days later, in the evening, a little boat made of bark and bamboo was taken down to the shore while young children ran around the village shouting, "The boat's about to go!"

Carrying the offerings of food from the altar, Isaku followed after his mother when she grabbed the bamboo rod and headed down to the beach. The little boat was set afloat down by the waterside, where Isaku and the other villagers loaded it with offerings of food. His mother stood her bamboo rod in the boat as well.

On the village chief's command, the bark and bamboo vessel was towed away from the shore by two boats and released about forty yards offshore. The two fishermen tossed their flaming torches into the little boat, which started to burn immediately. Engulfed in flames, it slowly drifted out to sea. They saw the white banner burn and fall. The spirits would make their journey back across the sea by the light of the burning boat.

The sea slipped into darkness as the flames gradually died down and eventually went out. Isaku and his mother stood on the beach for a long time.

Fine weather continued for days on end, and gigantic columns of clouds stretched out along the horizon. Occasionally the sky would abruptly turn dark and unleash furious squalls on the village.

His mother spent her days picking wild vegetables in the mountains with the other women or foraging for shellfish and seaweed down on the shore. Isaku noticed that at times she would sit motionless, staring blankly into space. Every time he saw his mother like this he remembered the sight of his father's body moving up and down on top of her in the darkness of the night. His father was silent, but his mother sounded as though she were being crushed to death. While it sounded like the groans of someone in agony, Isaku knew that she was in ecstasy.

Already a year and a half had passed since his father had

left. His mother had spent this time without experiencing any pleasure; no doubt she was recalling the last time she had been held by her husband. Weaving cloth to make something for his father to wear, she stopped the loom and silently caressed the cloth.

The summer heat abated and the nights became cooler. It was typical for rain to fall persistently in early autumn, and that year was no exception.

After about a month the sky turned a clear, lucent color and a cloudless blue sky unfolded. The sea was calm and the squid were biting.

Two men headed for the next village loaded with dried squid to trade for fishing gear such as hooks and spears. Five days later they returned with news from the labor contractor of villagers still in servitude. They had heard nothing of Isaku's father, but Tami's elder sister had died. It had happened six weeks earlier, and by all accounts she was cremated in the town where she had been working.

The following day fishing was called off, and Isaku joined the other villagers at Tami's house. In place of the body, the bowl and chopsticks that Tami's sister had used were placed inside the coffin as the old women of the village intoned the sutras.

The funeral procession formed and headed out. Isaku brought up the rear with a bundle of firewood on his back. Tami's family walked directly behind the coffin. They followed the path up the slope, through the forest, and into the clearing. There the coffin was laid in the crematory.

The fire was lit and flames consumed the coffin. The spirit was in the coffin even without the body, and would depart with the smoke to a place far off across the sea. The chanting of the sutras intensified, and Isaku pressed his palms together in prayer. Suddenly Tami burst into tears. Her hair was tied at the back, and loose strands blew in the wind. Isaku watched her from behind; her shoulders trembled as she sobbed. The villagers spent three days of mourning in their homes.

The time came for the women to go up to the narrow terraced fields to gather millet and other grains, which they would carry back in bags to their families, but the soil was stony and barren, yielding only the meagerest of crops. Isaku's mother went to their field and came back with a pitiful amount of grain to store away in their larder.

Down at the shore the men started catching autumn octopuses. Normally they began to appear about the time the eulalia grass came into ear, but this year they were coming into shore unusually early. Isaku put his boat out on the water among the rocks and occupied himself catching octopuses. He stopped working the oar and slipped the barbed spear with its red cloth into the water, moving it toward crannies in the rocks or clumps of seaweed. When an octopus mistook the waggling red cloth for food and showed itself, Isaku would hook it on the end of the spear. Before too long, around all the houses in the village, octopuses could be seen hanging out to dry in the sun.

The autumn winds began to blow, and when the ears of the eulalia grass reached their full length, the octopus catch dropped off noticeably. There was almost no sign of them, however much Isaku fluttered the red cloth. Even so, on the rare occasions he did see an octopus lured out toward the rag, he unerringly hooked it every time. Isaku thought his skills had improved since the previous autumn.

When he moved the spear around in the water, he remembered the saury fishing. His had been the smallest catch among the fishermen, but since it was only his second season, he was happy that he had reached the stage where he could grab the fish. He felt confident that as the years went by and he got more experience, he would eventually become a full-fledged fisherman.

The men were puzzled by the small octopus catch. Normally octopus would be dried and then sold off to merchants in the next village or to people in mountain villages for the New Year, in exchange for grain. The octopus was essential to acquire enough provisions to see them through winter, and a poor catch would have a serious effect on the village's food supply. An air of gloom set in among the fishermen.

Isaku's mother took his younger brother and sister on repeated trips into the forest to gather dry branches. In preparation for the coming winter, Isaku helped his mother cut these up into firewood to be stacked in a corner of the house.

He would often stop what he was doing out on the water and look over toward the far-off crests of the ridges. The chances that they would be blessed with a visitation were slim, but if one did come, there was no doubt that the villagers would be saved and the dark cloud cast over the village by the poor octopus catch would disappear in an instant.

One morning while sitting in his boat out on the water, Isaku noticed the faintest hint of change on the crest of the farthest ridge. The mountains were either covered in green or the color of bare rocks, but the green along that crest was somewhat different from the other ridges. It could only be the first sign that the autumn hues were on their way.

That evening, when Isaku returned home, he said to his mother, "The mountains look as if they're changing color." She kept chopping firewood, saying nothing, not even glancing in his direction. Maybe she had already noticed the

change on the ridge, or maybe she had half given up hope of
*O-fune-sama*'s visiting their shores that winter. Isaku could
not tell.

About two weeks later the crest of the ridge began to
turn red, and as the days went by it deepened in color and
eventually spread to the other ridges. Fleecy clouds drifted
across the otherwise clear sky, and there was a chill on the
water.

The autumn colors approached like wildfire, staining the
hills behind them before enveloping the village itself. In the
meantime it seemed that the little octopus had already left
the shoreline, to be seen no more.

Takichi's wife Kura was chosen to be the pregnant woman
for the *O-fune-sama* ritual. Her belly had started to swell
around the time the octopus first appeared in the shallows,
and with her conspicuous large frame, the village chief did
not hesitate to appoint her for the task.

That day, the villagers assembled on the beach. Her hair
combed and tied up behind her head, Kura wore a solemn
expression as she stepped into Takichi's boat. She appeared
especially large next to her slight husband.

Takichi took up the oar and worked the boat away from
the shore. Avoiding the places where the water foamed above
hidden rocks, he rowed the boat a little farther out before
finally stopping. Kura stood up and threw the sacred festoon
she had been holding into the sea. Isaku and the others
pressed their palms together in prayer as the boat turned back
to the shore.

They all followed Kura to the village chief's house.

The chief was sitting in orthodox style, his legs folded
under him as he welcomed her into the room. Kura knelt in
front of him and placed her hands on the floor as she bowed

deeply. Rising to her feet, she kicked the little square table placed in front of the village chief. It flew almost as far as the wall, the food in the bowl scattering on the floor. Kura was much more powerful than the woman Isaku had seen the previous year; she even drew murmurs of admiration from the men gathered in the entrance.

After adjusting her kimono she bowed again to the village chief and left with Takichi to go back to her own house.

That night Isaku was invited to represent his family at Takichi's house. Kura's selection for the O-fune-sama ritual was an auspicious occasion, and tradition held that her baby would grow up to be sturdy and strong. Kura's father was also there. Millet wine was brought out, and they were served bowls of dumpling soup. Takichi's mother was sitting hunched-over by the fireside.

"With your missus kicking the table across the room like that, people are saying that O-fune-sama could well be on the way," said Isaku, sipping on the wine in his bowl. If only a ship would capsize for them the way that table had been turned over, he thought.

"That'd be good all right," Takichi muttered.

Kura's father just sat there drinking his wine as his daughter poured some plain hot water into Takichi's mother's bowl. Takichi screwed up his face, flushed red from the wine. "We'll be in trouble if O-fune-sama doesn't come. The baby'll mean another mouth to feed. Maybe I'll have to do the same as your father and sell myself to keep them from starving," he said, looking at Isaku dolefully.

Isaku cringed, but it was hardly unexpected. Takichi was going to have to shoulder the burden of supporting not only his aged mother but also his wife Kura and the baby that was due before long. Being unable to sell the saury, and then the poor octopus catch on top of that, meant that Takichi's family had not been able to get any grain from the next village, putting them in dire straits.

Their situation was exactly the same as that of Isaku's family. Even though his father had been a skilled fisherman, a poor season had left him with no option but to sell himself into bondage. There was a limit to the food to be reaped from the sea, and every year the catch was getting smaller. If *O-fune-sama* did not grace their shores soon, there would likely be a flood of people leaving to go into bondage.

"I had to smack Kura once to set her straight. Said she'd go once the baby's weaned. She's big and could probably get a good price, but I'm not having any of that. No wife of mine's selling herself. It's me who's gotta go." Takichi's eyes glistened as he spoke. Kura's father said nothing, merely stared at the flames.

Isaku took a sip of the vegetable porridge Kura had served him, then took his leave. The wine made him feel unsteady on his feet. Tears started to flow down his cheeks as he made his way home. He understood how his father must have felt when he left his family behind. His parting words were "Don't let the children starve," but Teru had died. When his father had left, entrusting the well-being of the family to someone as untried as Isaku, he must have been well aware that a death among them was a very real possibility. His mother always tried to give the children as much food as she could, as she scooped the solids from the vegetable porridge into the children's bowls while she herself only drank the liquid. She knew how his father felt and was doing her best to keep the children alive.

He felt himself teetering in the wind off the sea, immersed in the sound of the waves.

He had only a vague memory of the last time *O-fune-sama* had visited their shores, but when he recalled that strangely festive atmosphere, he thought that it must be some treasure indeed to make the villagers go wild with joy.

He walked along the path toward the faint outline of his house against the light of the night sky.

5

The reds and yellows mantling the far-off ridges began to fade as the temperature dropped with each passing day. One morning when the sea was calm, Isaku stepped down to the earthen floor to be told by his mother, "Take Isokichi out with you from now on."

Isaku stared at his younger brother, who sat beside the fireplace facing him. In effect, she wanted him to teach Isokichi how to work an oar and catch fish. Though the boy had started to help carry bundles of dried branches home from the mountains behind their house, Isaku thought it would be a tough task to teach little Isokichi how to become a fisherman.

"Isokichi, why are you still sitting on your butt?" yelled his mother, slapping his little brother fiercely across the face. Isokichi got to his feet and scampered to the dirt floor, still holding his hand against his cheek. Isaku picked up the oar that stood in the corner of the room, swung it onto his shoulder, and left the house. His mother and Isokichi followed behind him, fishing tackle in hand. With the last hint of dawn still in the sky, there wasn't a cloud to be seen, holding promise of a clear autumn day.

As he walked to the shore he thought that it was about time Isokichi started going out on the water. Isaku had first been taken out by his father the spring of the year he turned seven, and Isokichi would reach the same age by New Year. With their father away, no doubt his mother wanted Isokichi to get accustomed to working out on the sea as soon as possible so he could start helping Isaku. Having spent all his time fishing alone since his father had left, Isaku thought that his brother would be little more than a millstone around his neck, yet he looked forward to being out on the water with him. He was proud to think that now he was teaching someone the ropes.

At the shore they slid the boat toward the water. Isokichi braced his legs as he pushed. Isaku attached the oar and worked the boat away from the water's edge. Their mother stood watching them for a short while before hurrying back to their house.

Isokichi sat cross-legged in the bottom of the boat, a sparkle in his eyes and a relaxed look on his face. For him, being able to go out on the water to learn how to fish was a joy beyond words.

"Come over here," said Isaku. Making his brother grasp the oar, he put his own hand on top and moved the oar in the water.

"You work the oar with your arm, not your hand," said Isaku. He adjusted Isokichi's feet and slapped him in the small of his back to get him into the right position. When they drew nearer to the foaming water around the rocks, Isaku took the oar from his brother's hand and maneuvered the boat himself.

"If you don't know how to turn the prow to change direction, you'll end up on the rocks. Keep your eyes on the way I work the oar." Isokichi nodded intently.

Isaku stopped the boat and dropped anchor before fixing some bait to a hook and line, which he then dropped over the side. There was nothing other than small fry to be caught, but these would be dried and stored to eat during winter. Whenever he felt a bite on the line, he would reel in the fish at just the right moment and seemed hardly ever to fail. Isokichi ran his hands over the little fish flapping around in the bottom of the boat.

Isaku plied the boat from one area of rocks to another, letting Isokichi take over the oar along the way, rowing with his hand placed on top.

From that day on, he spent his days with Isokichi out on the water. Isokichi did little more than work the oar and watch his older brother fish, but even this seemed to exhaust him. Almost right after dinner he would start to nod off and then lie down on his straw mattress.

The leaves on the trees started to dry up, and whirls of fallen leaves rose from the woods behind them to rain down on the village. The sea, too, began to show the first signs of winter, blustery nor'westers became commonplace, and the chill on the water intensified.

One day when the sea was calm, after they had been on the water two hours, a ship big enough to carry about four hundred bales appeared from behind the cape to the west, followed by another of about half that size; both disappeared off to the east. At this time of year freshly harvested rice was transported by ship, and the piles of cargo they could see on board were undoubtedly straw bales of rice.

The next day, on the instructions of the village chief, a

makeshift hut was erected on the beach in preparation for salt-making.

Calm weather continued, but three days later a strong wind started to blow, and spray from the waves smashing onto the shore rained on the houses close to the water. The boats were pulled up away from the water's edge and tied to stakes driven into the ground.

That night the first fires were lit under the salt cauldrons. On his way back from the outhouse Isaku stood and looked at the beach. The flames were being fanned by the wind, and he could see people moving. With no stars or moon in the sky, all that could be seen through the pitch-darkness was the dim white of the waves breaking near the fires. From time to time he could feel a mist on his face.

His mother joined the other women taking the salt from the cauldrons up to the village chief's house and carrying each household's contribution of firewood down to the beach. Isaku would take Isokichi out fishing on calm days, into the woods to collect dry branches for firewood on days when the sea was rough.

One windy day a calamity befell the village.

In the evening Kichizo had gone down to the beach to work on the cauldrons; when he returned the next morning, he discovered that his wife had disappeared. He searched for her throughout the village, down by the shore, and in the woods behind the houses, but she was not to be found. From the panicked look on his face his neighbors could tell that something had happened and told the village chief. When he was questioned by the chief, it became clear that he had been wickedly cruel to his wife the previous night.

Kichizo had never been able to rid himself completely of the suspicion that his wife had had a child by another man during her time away in servitude, and at times he still saw fit to torment her. This occasion was another example of his uncontrollable rage. It seemed that after beating his wife, he had hacked off pieces of her hair, tied her up, then gone so far as to shave off her pubic hair.

The village chief listened to the man's confession and concluded that Kichizo's wife must have been so terrified that she had run away during the night. He ordered several men to hurry to the next village.

They headed for the pass, but when they stopped to look around the graveyard, they found Kichizo's wife hanging by the neck from a tree not far from the crematory. They cut her body down, wrapped it in straw matting, and carried it back to Kichizo's house. Kichizo clung to his wife's body and wept.

Isaku and his mother went to pay their respects at the wake. The body had been bound tightly in a sitting position with rough twine, back against a funeral post. The three dark bruises he could see on her pallid face attested to the severe beating she had suffered. Her hair was hacked roughly and in places cropped almost down to the skin. Kichizo was kneeling in a corner of the room, head hanging forward. Normally the bodies of those who had taken their own lives would merely be thrown into the sea, but because her suicide had resulted from her fear of Kichizo's violence, the village chief granted special permission for her to be laid to rest in the cemetery.

The following day the body was placed in a coffin and carried to the cemetery, where it was cremated. Because it was said that the spirits of those who had killed themselves to settle a score were doomed to roam within the confines of the village, the village chief ordered that Kichizo should fast in his house for five days as penance, to allow his wife's spirit to leave for the place beyond the seas. But the night his wife was cremated, Kichizo slipped out of his house and hurled himself off a cliff near the cape. His head was caved in; one eyeball sat on top of his lips, and his brains spilled on the rocks. The villagers took his body out to sea and threw it in the water.

The death of Kichizo's wife left the people of the village stunned. Many chose to blame Kichizo and his vicious jealousy for having caused the tragedy; at the same time they gave credence to the rumor that Kichizo's wife had had a child by another man.

The sea became angry, and again the fires were lit under the salt cauldrons.

In early December Isaku's turn came to work through the night on the beach tending the fires. The wind wasn't so strong, but there was a great swell on the sea, immersing Isaku in the sound of the crashing waves as he added wood to the fires. In the clear light of the moon he could faintly see spray being hurled into the air where the low tide had exposed parts of the reef.

Isaku sat in the hut, warming himself by the fire as he watched the sea. All he could make out in the moonlight was the rising and falling of the waves, and despite all the stories, he couldn't imagine O-fune-sama ever actually coming.

On calm days he worked hard fishing, with Isokichi putting his all into the oar, never crying when he was slapped in the face for getting his foot positioning wrong or moving his back incorrectly. A mixture of blood and pus oozed from where the skin on his fingers and toes had split.

Their mother was asleep with their little sister in her arms, while Isaku and Isokichi lay down side by side. He reached out furtively and took hold of Isokichi's rough little hand as his brother snored away beside him. Isokichi was a very sound sleeper, and he usually had to be roughly shaken or even kicked awake by his mother at daybreak.

That year the snow arrived later than usual, but when the first snowfall did come, it fell with a vengeance, continuing for three days solid. The trees around the village were covered in snow, and icicles hung from the eaves of the houses.

One night at the end of December, Isaku had a dream. He could hear a voice from far off in the darkness, from out on the water. All of a sudden the voice was up close, and he was enveloped in the sound of the waves breaking on the beach. The waves bore down upon him, and he felt himself stagger. Then he heard a shrill voice calling his name right by his ear. It was his mother. She was hitting him about the head and kicking his shoulders.

He raised himself up on his arms. His mother slapped him across the face, screaming, her eyes open wide, as her face loomed out of the pale light from the last embers of the fire.

"O-fune-sama," she screamed.

He leaped out of bed. He could hear people's voices outside. He had no idea what to do.

"Get some wood on the fire!" said his mother to Isokichi, standing there drowsy-eyed.

"Grab an axe or something and get down to the beach," she shouted as she stepped onto the earthen floor, putting on her straw raincoat and sedge hat. Isaku did the same as he picked up his rusty gaff.

He burned with excitement. His heart raced at the thought that the long-awaited O-fune-sama had actually arrived. If it was a ship fully loaded with cargo, they would be able to procure not just grain but rice. He remembered the sweet taste of the tiny amount of white sugar his mother had given him when he was sick as a baby.

Isaku ran out the door after his mother, who had swung

a mattock on her shoulder. The sky bristled with stars, casting a pale light over the path through the snow. His body was shaking uncontrollably, and his knees felt as if they were going to give out under him.

Villagers were running down the path as Isaku stepped onto the beach. He could see people gathered around the cauldron fires. A mass of wood was being fed under the cauldrons, and sparks shot into the air as the fire blazed. Some people were holding up flaming torches, illuminating the scene just enough for Isaku to make out the village chief's face.

"Where's O-fune-sama?" asked his mother.

"Right out in front here. She's listing to one side. Definitely ripped her belly open on the rocks," replied one of the men, his voice shaking as he spoke.

Isaku looked out to sea. The dull white crests of the waves surged in, and cold spray rained down on them each time the breakers smashed on the shore. As his eyes became gradually accustomed to the dark, he could make out by the light of the stars what looked to be quite a large ship. The ship was leaning over to one side, veiled in spray from the waves.

The inside of his mouth felt dry. Struggling to make any headway in the rough seas, no doubt they had mistaken the fires on the beach for the lights of houses and had turned the helm in toward the shore, only to smash onto the reef. This was Isaku's first sight ever of O-fune-sama. The thought came into his mind that maybe Kura's role in the O-fune-sama ritual had paid off after all.

Isaku felt an urge to yell at the top of his lungs, but the village chief and the others stood silently as they looked out to sea. With the arrival of O-fune-sama their prayers had finally been answered, and it seemed strange to Isaku that no one was jumping for joy. Bewildered, he cast furtive glances at the faces of those around him.

"What about the crest on the sails?" he heard someone ask in a penetrating voice.

"That's what we don't know. The wind's so strong they've shortened sail. And it's dark. Can't see a thing," said an irritated voice from near the cauldrons.

Isaku finally understood why they were all so quiet, and felt ashamed of himself for not realizing earlier. The crest on the sails would tell them whether the ship belonged to a clan or was a merchant vessel. What they were longing for was a merchant ship, with its promise of bounty for the village. But if it was a clan ship, plundering cargo would be out of the question. If they stepped an inch out of line, they would all be severely punished.

"Kura's not here yet?" asked the village chief, buffeted by the wind.

"She should be here soon," replied the man standing at his side. The village chief had asked her to come to the beach again as the pregnant woman, and no doubt he would have her pray that the ship out there was a merchant vessel.

"Here she is!" said a voice from the crowd as Kura stepped onto the beach and walked toward the village chief with Takichi, who was holding a flaming torch in his hand. Her belly was large and her movements were labored.

Kura bowed to the village chief, took the sacred straw festoon from him, and held it reverently in front of her before walking over to the water's edge and casting it into the sea. The sound of the sutras rose from the crowd, and Isaku joined them in prayer.

The cold intensified, and the men took turns feeding wood to the fires under the cauldrons. On the village chief's instructions, more wood was brought down and another fire was lit, around which the villagers stood warming themselves.

The wind died down slightly as the first signs of dawn appeared. The night sky took on a bluish tinge, and the stars began to fade. The villagers fixed their eyes on the sea. Fountains of spray shot into the air around each side of the reef, and there, on one such cluster of rocks, for all to see was a ship stuck hard and fast. It swayed ever so slightly each time it was pounded by the waves.

"She holds two hundred bales."

"More like three hundred," the men whispered. The sails had been lowered, and the crests could not be seen.

"She's got a full load."

There was no doubt the deck was packed with what appeared to be cargo. Normally, if the crew sensed they might be in danger of sinking, they would cut the cargo free and jettison it overboard to stabilize the ship, but most likely they had spotted the lights on the shore and turned to land.

The sky became lighter, and the outline of the ship was clearly visible. The canvas of the shortened sails flapped in the wind.

"I can see the crest," said someone in a low voice.

"It's not the daimyo's crest. It's a merchant ship!" cried one of the men.

For a moment there was silence, then suddenly the villagers broke into cheers. The crests of clan ships were large and were found in the middle of the sails, but the ship listing before them out on the water had only a small crest at the very top of the sail.

Isaku was shouting ecstatically with the rest of them.

The early-morning shore resounded with something halfway between cheering and wailing. There were people literally jumping for joy, while others ran around kicking up snow.

Isaku heard the sound of crying behind him; several women standing in a huddle were sobbing, no doubt overcome by the pain and sadness in their lives, lives never free from the fear of starvation. Tears welled up in Isaku's eyes, too. If his father had not sold himself into bondage, maybe his sister would not have died.

"Be quiet!" snapped the tall elder standing alongside the village chief. "Out on O-fune-sama, there's people out there."

Silence reigned as the villagers stood motionless, their eyes on the ship, the upper part of which protruded from the shimmering sea. There were people on board all right, sitting at the base of the main mast, palms pressed in prayer as they looked toward shore.

"The village chief has asked me to take over. I'll give the orders from now. Calm down and do as I say. First of all, we need lookouts. Gonsuke!" A man with one arm stepped toward the cauldrons.

"As always, you're in charge of lookouts. I want them on Tide and Crow Points. And don't miss a thing!" said the old man, drilling Gonsuke with a steely look. Gonsuke bowed, turned to the villagers, and said, "Kinta, help us this time, too." A small man emerged from the crowd and stood beside Gonsuke.

"Sahei, Isaku. You've got young eyes. Go on lookout with Gonsuke and Kinta," the elder said.

Isaku was not only disappointed at being assigned a job not involving the disposal of the wrecked ship, but also annoyed because he very much wanted to see what the villagers did with the long-awaited O-fune-sama. He followed Sahei over toward Gonsuke.

"Right, let's get going. Get as much rope as you can. Also

axes, mattocks, and mallets." With this the villagers hurried up the slope back to their houses. As though girding himself for action, the old man took a handkerchief from his belt and wrapped it around his head.

Gonsuke explained the role of lookout to Isaku and Sahei. At sea there would be two types of ships passing, those that sailed in deep water and those that hugged the coastline. If the people aboard the latter were to see them disposing of O-fune-sama, the villagers would be severely punished for plundering cargo. The lookouts were to keep watch from the promontories jutting out into the sea. If they spotted a ship, they were to use a signal fire as a warning, and the village chief would immediately stop the work dismantling the ship.

"I was chosen because I'm farsighted. Kinta's got good eyes, too. It's an important job. You've got to keep your eyes peeled, too," said Gonsuke. Kinta and Sahei would go on lookout on Tide Point to the west, and Gonsuke and Isaku on the Crow Point to the east.

With daybreak came the first signs of sun rising behind the snow-covered mountains to the rear of the village. The wind had died, but there was still a considerable swell on the sea. The ship was now clearly visible, its broad rudder smashed in half, and the railings on the starboard side must have been blasted clean off the deck by the force of the waves. Two men could be seen sitting beside the mast, their hands together in prayer as they looked toward the shore.

Isaku did as Gonsuke ordered and ran back to his house, put some roasted beans into a bag, and tied it to his belt. His mother must have been at the village chief's house because there was no sign of her or his little sister.

He slipped a hatchet under his waistband and hurried out of the house up the path, where he met Gonsuke waiting

with an axe over his shoulder at the start of the mountain
trail. The two of them followed the trail through the deep
snow before climbing up a rocky slope. The farther they
climbed, the more they could hear the cawing of crows and
see birds resting their wings in the treetops. Gonsuke was
fleet of foot, and Isaku sweated profusely as he struggled to
keep up.

Soon they reached the top of the promontory. This was
the first time Isaku had set foot there. Gonsuke plowed his
way through the snow, threading a path ahead between the
low trees. Down below they could hear the thunderous waves
breaking on the rocks.

The wooded part of the point came to an end, and they
stepped out into a flat, open area. They stood at the very tip
of the cape, looking down to the left at the village and across
the bay. They could see the water seething white around the
reef, and they had a clear view of the wrecked ship. It was
an excellent spot to post a lookout. Across the bay was Tide
Point, also covered in snow as it jutted out into the sea. Isaku
imagined Sahei hurrying with Kinta toward its tip.

"Get some dead trees and branches together," Gonsuke
said hurriedly.

Isaku followed the man back into the trees, then started
dragging out dead pieces of wood and carrying bundles of dry
branches. Gonsuke meanwhile used his hatchet to strip pieces
of bark from tree trunks.

Gonsuke lit a fire, adding some dry branches to the pile
once the wood caught alight. Isaku worked with the axe cutting up branches.

"If you put snow on these pieces of bark and then put
them on the fire, it works as a smoke signal. You keep watch,"
said Gonsuke.

The sea glistened in the sunlight; not a bird could be seen in the clear sky. Isaku flinched from the cold wind off the water and moved to the fire, keeping his eyes on the sea.

"They've started," said Gonsuke. Isaku looked down at the bay. He could see many small boats setting off from the shore toward the wrecked ship. There was a crowd on the beach.

"Keep your eyes out to sea," barked Gonsuke, but he, too, was looking down into the bay. The fleet of small boats converged on the stranded ship, eventually surrounding it, just like a horde of ants around a caterpillar. Several boats drew up alongside the ship, and he could see people climbing on board. He thought that no doubt they would be screaming at the ship's crew, but the sunbathed cove felt eerily tranquil.

The boats stayed around the ship for some time before starting to ferry what seemed to be cargo from the ship's deck back to shore. This activity grew more and more hectic as the little boats plied to and fro between the ship and the shore.

The lifeless sails were removed and the mast was cut down and dropped into the sea, throwing up a sheet of spray as it hit the water. One of the boats worked its way to the floating mast and proceeded to tow it to shore. The cargo was stacked up on the beach and looked to be very much like straw bales of rice.

Feeling hungry, Isaku started eating some of the roasted beans he had in his bag.

"There's quite a bit of cargo there. That's some haul," said Gonsuke, his voice trembling as he looked down on the bay.

"Is this more than O-fune-sama in the past?" asked Isaku.

"There have been bigger ships, but this amount of cargo's

unusual. There's a lot on the beach, and there's still more to come off the ship." Gonsuke's eyes glistened with excitement.

Gonsuke undoubtedly knew what he was talking about, since he had been on lookout each time *O-fune-sama* had come. Isaku felt the excitement welling up inside him at the very thought of the exceptional amount of cargo. "What do you think could be on board?" he asked.

"Well, first of all, there could be rice, then maybe things like beans, cloth, pottery, tobacco, writing paper, oil, and sugar. Once there was even a ship carrying twenty casks of wine," he said, baring his chipped teeth as he grinned.

The ship must have been finally emptied of cargo around the time the sun began to set. The boats became less active, and the villagers started to carry everything off the beach up to the chief's house.

The snow on the mountains looming behind the village took on a purple tinge before giving way to the night. Down on the beach the light of the fire suddenly glimmered, and the village sank into darkness.

Isaku helped Gonsuke dig a hole into the deep snow that had built up behind a large rock, lining the inside with dry leaves and grass. After they crisscrossed sticks over the top of the hole and placed bark on top, they climbed in and lay down back to back.

There was a wicked chill in the air, but inside the hole it gradually became warmer. Gonsuke started to snore.

Isaku lay in the dark, his eyes wide open. By all accounts the village chief would order the bounty from *O-fune-sama* to be distributed fairly to each household, according to the number of people in each family. With the bulk of the cargo undoubtedly being bales of rice, Isaku was beside himself with joy at the thought of partaking of such a delicacy. His younger brother and sister had never tasted rice, and he imagined the luxury of serving them rice gruel. He could just picture how the delectably sweet taste of the white gruel would astonish them.

Gonsuke was certainly right about the large haul, and naturally this meant that each family could look forward to receiving a generous amount of food and other items. With the saury not selling and a poor catch of autumn octopus allowing them to buy only a pitiful amount of grain, the coming of O-fune-sama was nothing less than deliverance from the fear of starvation. If managed properly, the bounty would last them two or even three years. There would be no need for them to sell themselves into bondage, and no doubt they would be able to lead quiet, peaceful lives for some time to come. Tami would stay with her family, and Takichi would continue to spend his days as a fisherman and a father to his child.

Isaku put his hand over his heart. The coming of O-fune-sama was due to divine intercession, and Isaku wanted to offer a prayer of gratitude from the bottom of his heart.

The sound of the waves breaking at the foot of the promontory seemed to reverberate from the earth's very core. Before he knew it he was asleep.

He woke up to a hand jostling his shoulder.

Gonsuke reached up and pushed aside the branches and bark covering the hole. Isaku felt a sudden rush of cold air. There were still stars in the night sky, but they were losing their brightness.

Isaku crawled out of the hole. Gonsuke was blowing some life into the dying embers of the fire, and in no time he had the dry branches crackling.

Isaku warmed himself by the fire as he looked out to sea. As daybreak drew near, the sea was calm. Down in the bay, work had already started; he could see what must have been flaming torches set up in the boats moving on the water, as well as on the stranded ship.

Gonsuke cooked two salted saury in the fire, handing one to Isaku. Fat oozed out of the hot fish, and as he ate it with the roasted beans, the saltiness of the saury was neutralized, producing an incredibly delicious taste.

Daybreak came, and the sea was bathed in morning sunlight. Splashes of spray shot up again and again around the stranded ship as pieces of timber and planks were thrown overboard.

"Looks like they're taking O-fune-sama apart," said Isaku, straining his eyes to see what was happening.

"That's because she's made of good-quality timber. Can be used for anything. There's nails and hinges to be had there, too. And all the pots and pans down in the galley, not to mention the knives, buckets, and rice tubs. Sometimes there's even cabinets or chests," said Gonsuke enthusiastically.

Now Isaku understood why the elder in charge had got them to prepare saws, axes, and mallets. The ship was being taken apart and the timber dropped into the water.

The boats were towing it to the shore, where it was being pulled up on the beach. From there it was carried into the woods behind the village.

Isaku and Gonsuke cast their eyes across the sea: no sign of any passing vessels. Off to the east, they could now see scores of seabirds dancing in the air like snowflakes, with the reflections off a school of fish breaking the surface of the sea below them. No smoke was to be seen over the other side of the bay, either, on Tide Point.

Two small boats started to move away from the ship in the direction of the promontory where Isaku and Gonsuke were standing.

"They're taking the bodies away," said Gonsuke.

Isaku looked over. He could clearly see something covered with straw matting in the bottom of the boats. Eventually, the boats started to disappear from sight, one after another, down at the foot of the cape.

The tumult around the ship showed no signs of stopping, and the vessel soon lost all semblance of its original shape. Work was progressing at a brisk pace, and already the part of the stern that held the smashed rudder had disappeared. He could see a boat carrying away the sailcloth.

Just after the Hour of the Horse, the only part remaining on the rocks was the bottom of the hull. There were also people actually standing on the reef as they worked on the boat with astonishing speed.

When the timber from what seemed to be bunks was towed away, all that was left floating on the water were pieces of the keel. When these were pulled up onto the shore, the last trace of the ship disappeared from the rocky bay, leaving nothing but the placid sea.

"Have you ever seen a ship heading this way when you've been on lookout?" asked Isaku, seeming to lose interest in the task at hand.

"Yeah, I have. Two in one day," said Gonsuke, scanning the sea.

A plume of smoke rose into the air.

"That's the signal that they've finished. That's it for us, too," said Gonsuke, throwing snow on the fire. "Let's go and have a look at what they've got. Looks like a fair-sized haul all right," he added, swinging his axe up onto his shoulder.

Isaku followed Gonsuke into the woods, weaving his way

between the trees as he scampered to keep up with Gonsuke's fast clip. Exhilarated, he felt as if he were walking on air. No doubt his mother and Isokichi had worked through the day with the other villagers.

He wanted to be part of the frenzied excitement in the village as quickly as he could. When they reached the mountain path, Gonsuke, axe on his back, broke into a trot with Isaku close behind, impatient to see the bounty O-fune-sama had brought.

Coming out of the trees they could see the shore down to the right. They expected to see the villagers dancing madly, but instead they all stood stock-still by the water's edge. Taken aback, Isaku broke stride for a second, but with Gonsuke running on unperturbed down the slope he followed after him.

Gonsuke left the path and stepped onto the beach. Breathing hard, Isaku walked over to the gathering.

The villagers were standing around their chief, palms pressed together as they faced out to sea. Isaku finally understood that they were offering prayers of gratitude for the bounty bestowed on them by the sea. When the village chief finished praying, the elder standing beside him turned to the people and in a spirited voice said, "Well done. Your hard work has made your chief happy. Now go home and spend the rest of the day praying to your ancestors. The bounty from O-fune-sama will be apportioned tomorrow morning."

The chief left the water's edge, followed by the villagers, no one saying a word, the glint in their eyes and their beaming smiles telling all. Prodded by Gonsuke, Isaku took a step in front of the elder. The old man was satisfied when Gonsuke reported that there had been no signs of ships approaching. Isaku bowed deeply and walked to his house.

When Isaku pushed his way past the straw matting

hanging at the doorway, his mother turned to look at him as she prayed in front of the *ihai*, their ancestral tablet. She looked completely different, her face flushed with happiness, the corners of her mouth turned upward in a way that Isaku had never seen in her before.

He stepped onto the floor, pressed his palms together in front of the ancestral tablet, and sat down by the fireside. Feeling another wave of joy, he wanted to jump up and dance around the room.

The sun had begun to go down and the temperature was falling. His mother started heating a pot of water with buckwheat seeds, then brought some salted saury over to the fireside. Obviously the makings of a meal much more generous than usual.

"What was on *O-fune-sama?*" Isaku asked his mother.

"Rice, and lots of it," his mother said, enunciating each word for effect.

"What else?"

"There was cotton and rapeseed oil, too. Wax, tea, wine and soy sauce, vinegar and matting. But the rice . . . This *O-fune-sama* was a rice ship," said his mother excitedly.

What a great day it is, Isaku thought. It was a joy to see his mother so talkative, and he felt her happiness affecting not only him but his brother and sister as well; they sat, smiling, beside him. When the buckwheat seeds started to dance in the hot water, his mother added some vegetables and seaweed. The room grew dark, and their faces gleamed red in the light from the flames. Smoke started to float up from the skewered saury around the fire. His mother filled their bowls from the pot one by one, Isaku first, next his brother, and then his sister, before serving herself.

Isaku nibbled on a saury and sipped away at the vegetable

porridge. The next day the rice would be distributed, and he was elated at the thought of his brother and sister's first taste of rice gruel.

"Just another year and a bit more now," whispered his mother as she picked up her bowl. Isaku looked at her, wondering what she meant, but soon realized from the gleam in her eyes that she was thinking of his father. He had gone into bondage for a three-year term, which would be up around the time the snow melted the year after next. Some of the bounty from *O-fune-sama* would undoubtedly still be left, which would take a load off his father's mind. If they were starving, his father might even consider selling himself into bondage once again; but now such fears were gone.

His mother dished out another serving of vegetable porridge for his brother and sister, a relaxed expression on her face as she manipulated her chopsticks. Shortly after finishing the meal, his little sister started to nod off, so his mother picked her up and carried her to the straw bedding. His brother lay down in the corner of the room.

"How many dead bodies were there?" asked Isaku, remembering the two little boats he had seen from his observation post on the cape.

His mother looked up as she sipped on her cup of hot water.

"Three fell overboard and drowned. There were four people left on the ship, counting the injured men, but they were all killed," she said quietly.

"Did they resist at all?" asked Isaku as he watched his mother's face by the light of the fire.

"I heard they didn't do a thing, just pleaded for their lives," said his mother in a toneless voice.

Most likely the crew had cut off their topknots as they

sought divine protection. Isaku could imagine them kneeling on the deck, disheveled hair hanging down as they pleaded with the villagers to spare their lives.

"There's no room for pity. It'd be a disaster if any of 'em were allowed to live. They had to be killed, your ancestors decided that, and that's how it's been ever since. Village rules have to be obeyed," said his mother, a stony look in her eyes. Isaku nodded solemnly.

The next day the sea was rough. The waves broke on the shore with a thunderous roar, and the straw matting at the entrance to the houses fluttered as the wind lashed against the coast.

Isaku and his mother headed along the path to the village chief's house, spray raining down on them each time a wave crashed in. The faces of the people they met along the way beamed with joy.

The earthen floor of the entrance to the village chief's house thronged with people talking in restrained voices, but there was no doubting the gleam in their eyes and the gaiety in their voices. At the back of the room the village elders were busy laying out hemp stalks on the floor to use for their calculations. It had been decided that the rice would be distributed first.

The men bent over the sticks on the floor looked up as one of them got down on all fours and spoke to the village chief. The chief nodded again and again. When the trusted elder sitting beside the chief stood up, the noise of talk died away.

"There were three hundred and twenty-three bales of rice onboard O-fune-sama," he said. The crowd seemed to sway as one in reaction to his words. Isaku's heart almost missed a beat at the news of such incredible riches.

"Each adult man and woman will receive three bales and one bale for each child. The remaining forty-nine bales will be stored as the village chief's share."

On hearing this, the villagers struggled to hold back their excitement, and a hubbub of voices broke from the floor again as people bowed deeply toward the village chief.

Smiles appeared on the faces of the village chief and the elder, and Isaku saw his mother and others around him weeping. Those ten years old and above were judged to be adults, so both Isaku and his mother qualified for the adult quota. Isaku counted up their allotment on his fingers, working out that their family was entitled to eight bales of rice.

"We'll get eight bales!" he blurted excitedly to his mother.

"Eight bales!" she cried, looking down at her son. Tears continued to well up in her eyes and flow down her cheeks. From the look on her face, she seemed to be struggling to stop herself from breaking down and sobbing.

When people returned to the village from indentured service, the chief would supply them with their share of rice from what was stored away. When Isaku's father returned in the spring the year after next, he would receive an allotment, too, and the family would benefit even more.

The village chief got to his feet, as did the elder. The villagers followed them to the area behind the house. There were too many bales to fit in the storeroom, so they had been stacked up outside on straw matting. Isaku peered over people's shoulders at the bales of rice as though he were looking at an incredible treasure.

On the elder's instructions the men started dividing the bales of rice. Using hemp stalks, they counted the number of bales. When the elder called Isaku's name, eight bales of rice were laid on the ground with two long sticks, and two short ones signifying his brother and sister's allocation. He thought that if his sister Teru had not died, another short stick would have been placed there.

When the allocation was finished, the villagers prostrated themselves in front of the chief and uttered words of gratitude. Many pressed their hands together in prayer.

The elder raised his voice to be heard.

"Eat the rice a little at a time. We don't know when O-fune-sama will be back again. It might not be for years. People who get too used to the taste of rice will reap the consequences. You men must keep yourselves busy fishing, and the women must still scour the shore for shellfish."

The villagers bowed deeply once more.

They all got to their feet and stood in front of their respective allotments of rice, sixteen portions in all. Household heads took to the village path with their share.

"You'll never be able to carry that," said his mother. Isaku grabbed the rope on the bale and tried to lift it onto his shoulder, but could get it no further than his waist. It was much heavier than he had expected.

"Sissy!" barked his mother, but the smile on her face betrayed her happiness. She took hold of the bale and worked it up onto her shoulder, her hips wobbling a little as she set off along the path.

Isaku blushed with embarrassment, miserable to think that he, the supposed provider of the family, was unable to lift a bale of rice up onto his shoulder; what was more, his newfound fishing skills obviously counted for nothing when judging manhood, a humbling fact.

His mother made several trips between the village chief's house and their home, where they stacked up the bales on top of some planking on the earthen floor area. After carrying back the last bale, she took a drink of water, wiped the sweat from her brow, and sat down to have a rest before scooping a little bowlful of rice from one of the bales and placing it as an offering in front of the *ihai*, the ancestral tablet. The children copied their mother as she knelt in prayer.

In the evening his mother put the rice from the offering into a pot and started to boil it. The smell drifted up and brought to mind his last memories of rice as he stared at the seething white mass in the pot where the swollen grains jumped up and down. His mother served him some of the rice gruel. He was overwhelmed as soon as he put it to his lips: a rich and elegant taste. He felt as though he were being filled with strength. His little brother and sister ate speechlessly, but there was no mistaking the astonished look in their eyes.

Kura's father came to meet Isaku's mother and accompanied her to Takichi's house. Because Kura had played her role so successfully in the *O-fune-sama* ritual, she was now being lauded in the village. A celebration was held in her honor at Takichi's house.

A while later Isaku's mother returned home in high spirits.

"She did well. The village chief sent three bales of rice and some wine. He said that her kicking over that table so well was what brought *O-fune-sama* in." His mother had obviously been drinking, as she took a deep breath after gulping down some water from the jug.

The roar from crashing waves sounded oppressive to the ear, but it could not dampen the gaiety that prevailed throughout the village.

Isaku lay down to sleep beside Isokichi.

The distribution of goods continued the next day.

Rapeseed oil, soy sauce, vinegar, and wine were apportioned according to the size of each family, and the people carried away their shares in jars and tubs. The wax and half of the tea were to be kept at the village chief's house, which also functioned as the village meetinghouse. The tatami matting, too, was stored away.

That night the fires under the salt cauldrons were lit again because the village chief wanted to encourage his people to return to their daily routine, lest their windfall make them succumb to indolence. Even so, they hoped they might be blessed with yet another *O-fune-sama.*

The men started to go out fishing again on calm days, exchanging cheery glances across the water. Some even waved or smiled at Isaku without any special reason.

Isaku took Isokichi out on the water, but the thought of the bales of rice and the other luxuries piled up at home caused him to slacken. There were times when he pulled the line only to find that the bait had been taken. With enough food to last them a long time, Isaku lost the hunger needed to fish for small fry.

Even the women foraging for shellfish and seaweed on the shore seemed to spend more time chatting than working. Their cackling laughter could occasionally be heard out on the water.

Isaku's turn came to tend the fires on the beach. He had thought that *O-fune-sama* had always been little more than a pipe dream for the villagers, but now that he had experienced it firsthand, he felt the importance of the work on the cauldron fires and wanted nothing more than to see *O-fune-sama* out there when he was on duty.

The year ended, and New Year's Day came. Isaku turned eleven years of age.

As was the custom, during the New Year's holiday villagers stayed at home. Isaku spent his time in silence with his family. The sea was rough, and each day saw another snow squall. Their return to work on the sixth day of the New Year was marked by clear skies with little wind, but the sea was still running high. His mother put a generous amount of rice into the pot to boil. Pieces of dried squid grilled slowly on the fire. There was also a plateful of pickled octopus.

Isaku sipped on his gruel with its ample measure of rice and nibbled away at the dried squid. This was the first time he had partaken of a breakfast befitting New Year.

After the meal, they all went to pay their respects at the graves of their ancestors. So much snow had fallen that it came up to his hips. His mother had his little sister strapped to her back as she made her way with the other villagers to the cemetery. They brushed the snow off the graves, placed several grains of rice on each stone, and prayed.

They trudged back through the snow along the path to the village chief's house. The sky was blue and the glare off the snow was dazzling.

On stepping into the village chief's house they saw three of the more prominent members of the community sitting around, drinking wine. Isaku and his family bowed as they uttered New Year's greetings to the village chief, who smiled back and nodded in recognition.

When they got home, his mother poured Isaku some wine from a jar. He put it to his lips and felt its warmth spread through his mouth.

His mother took a sip. "It's good stuff. I've never had anything like this before. Wine made from rice is so much different," she said, shaking her head in wonderment. The full-bodied wine not only made Isaku feel hot all over but also put him in a buoyant mood.

"Next spring Father'll be back. I hope he comes back fit and well," said Isaku to his mother, who quickly turned around.

"Don't be so stupid! Of course he'll come back fit and well. Your father's a cut above any normal man. He's not the sort who gets sick," she said angrily.

Isaku held a sip of wine in his mouth. Thoughts of how he wanted to become a good fisherman before his father came back to the village passed through his mind. Also strong enough to lift easily one of those bales of rice.

The wine started to go to his head, and everything seemed to be swaying. Drinking the rest of his wine in one gulp, he staggered over to his straw bedding and lay down. He was asleep in no time at all.

When he woke up, the room was almost in darkness. The smell of rice gruel cooking hung in the air, and he could see his little brother and sister sitting beside the fire.

His mother stepped over to the ancestral table and lit the wick protruding from a dish containing some oil. His brother and sister stood up and moved over to the little platter, their eyes glued to the light. It was luminous. Isaku raised himself up and gazed at the light, a thin plume of smoke drifting from its flickering flame.

The gay atmosphere in the village continued beyond New Year. Wine in hand, the men would visit each other's houses for drinking parties, while the women indulged in chatting over tea. There was even talk of an old man who had said he would happily meet his maker now that he had tasted white sugar.

Every time his mother heard about how other families were steaming their rice and eating it, she would shake her head and frown.

"These things don't last forever. Those who aren't strong-minded in fortunate times will be the ones crying in the end," she muttered, as though telling herself as much as anyone else. In their house the rice was used sparingly, and only in gruel.

Even on calm days they saw fewer ships passing by. Most of the rice shipments would be made before the end of the year, and it was rare now for a ship to set sail and risk stormy seas. Not too long after New Year they sighted a large vessel, clearly a clan ship from its crest in the middle of the sail, as it tossed and pitched its way across the horizon before disappearing behind the cape.

At the end of January, Kura gave birth to a girl. Takichi had wanted a boy, and at first seemed disappointed. But he soon came around when the village chief not only gave them a gift of rice and wine but named the baby Tama, or jewel.

Isaku went with his mother to Takichi's house; she carried a bowl containing a handful of rice. There was a sacred straw festoon hanging in the doorway, and the baby was lying asleep beside Kura on the tatami matting lent to them by the village chief. Isaku's mother put the bowl down in front of the baby, where several other offerings had been placed, and then pressed her hands together in prayer. It was said that the souls of dead ancestors would return from across the sea to take shelter in the wombs of pregnant women in the village. Kura's newborn was therefore the reincarnation of such an ancestor: hence the relatives gathering to give offerings.

Isaku sat beside his mother with the other relatives around the fire. They exchanged celebratory greetings and filled each other's cups with wine. Isaku's mother seemed to be thinking of Teru, who had died a year earlier, as she cast her eyes toward the baby. It was said that many years were needed before reincarnation could come about, so no doubt Teru would now still be in the tranquillity offered by death.

The relatives talked about how Kura's performance in the ritual was the reason for the village's having been blessed with O-fune-sama and how joyous an occasion it was to have the village chief naming the baby.

"Tama's certainly lucky to be born when we've got rice from O-fune-sama. If she eats rice, she won't get sick; she'll grow up healthy," said one of the relatives to nods of agreement from those listening. Kura looked contented as she lay resting on her side.

The salt-making continued, and Isaku took his turn spending the night tending the fires on the beach in the middle of a snowstorm. In the morning, after he put out the fires under the cauldrons, some women came down to the shore carrying wooden tubs. Tami was among them.

Isaku watched as the women scooped the salt from the cauldrons and into the tubs. His eyes naturally focused on Tami's body. Her face had become long and thin, and it seemed she had grown a little taller. She was slender now but more solid around the hips, and had suddenly taken on a more womanly air.

A painful stifling feeling came over him. Isaku knew that Takichi had had relations with Kura when they had happened to meet in the forest, and he longed to approach Tami in the same way. But he could not imagine himself able to get near Tami, let alone speak to her if the opportunity did arise.

Tami attached two tubs full of salt to her bucket yoke and walked off through the snow toward the village chief's house. Isaku put out the fire in the little hut and made his way up the path from the beach.

With no more ships passing by, salt-making lost its meaning. The village was buried in deep snow. At times Isaku and his family would try to warm themselves against the freezing cold by sitting with their backs to the fire. A straw mat hung in the entranceway; by morning it would be as stiff as a board and frozen to the doorposts, so they would have to beat it with a stick to get it free.

Once February came the cold became a little less severe and the sea was calm for several days at a time. When the first sightings of plum blossom were made up in the mountains, the village chief ordered the salt-making stopped. The season for *O-fune-sama* had come to an end.

6

The first signs of spring grew more pronounced as the days passed and the snow covering the village started to melt. The houses shuddered as snow slid off the roofs. Steam floated up from the wet straw of the thatched roofs.

With the coming of spring people became more lively. As the temperature rose the fish came nearer to shore, too, and shellfish started to appear among the rocks. Each household's stock of rice meant that there was no shortage of grain, and with the fruits of the sea also ripe for picking, the villagers could eat well indeed.

Isaku noticed the change in people's faces. A look of contentment replaced the stern expression in their eyes. Some men sat in the sun in front of their houses smoking, while others lay idly on the shore.

Isaku heard that some of the villagers were secretly talking about a trip to sell salt to neighboring villages. A middle-aged man Isaku met on the path looked dolefully up toward

the mountain path and muttered, "I wonder if we have to go
and sell salt this year, too?"

Every year, at the end of February, the salt made during
the winter would be carried to the next village and exchanged
for grain. But with bales of rice stacked up in each household,
there was no need to go selling salt for a measly amount of
grain.

The salt was heavy, and carrying it up the mountain path
and over the pass was an unenviable task. People had slipped
and broken their legs, and even walking from sunrise to sunset, it took a full three days to reach the next village.

Isaku's mother would go from his family, and even she
frowned silently when Isaku said, "Seems quite a few people
say they don't want to sell salt."

One day when the sea was running high, Isaku made his
way to the village chief's house, where a meeting was to be
held. The earthen floor area was full of men and women. The
village chief was sitting at the fireside, and beside him was
the elder, who rose to his feet and stood in front of them.

"Those chosen to sell salt will leave at dawn tomorrow.
I hear, though, that some of you don't want to go. Do you
realize how stupid that would be? We go every year. What
would the people in the next village think if we didn't this
year? No doubt they'd think we'd got hold of something that
meant we didn't need any grain. It'd soon be known that
O-fune-sama had blessed us with her bounties. Didn't that
occur to you?" The old man's voice bristled with rage.

The faces of those assembled took on an ashen look as
they nodded solemnly.

The elder silently surveyed the villagers before saying,
"You'll leave tomorrow morning. The only food you'll take
with you will be millet dumplings and dried fish. Not one

grain of rice! Don't do anything to suggest that we're not on the brink of starvation." The old man's eyes again took on a steely glint as he returned to his position by the fire.

The villagers dispersed and Isaku headed home. He told his mother about the elder's speech and then said, "I'll go this year."

"A weakling like you carry salt?" his mother snapped.

The humiliation Isaku had felt when he had been unable to lift the bale of rice returned. His mother had laughed when she had called him a sissy, but this time he could sense contempt and annoyance in the word "weakling."

The next morning his mother got up at the Hour of the Ox (about 2:00 A.M.), made some millet dumplings, and wrapped them in seaweed along with some dried saury. At the Hour of the Tiger (about 4:00 A.M.) she put on her shoes, picked up a stout walking stick, and left the house.

Isaku stood in front of the door and watched the line of people emerge from the village chief's house and head off on their journey to sell salt. The sky turned a shade of blue. With bales of salt on their backs, the people steadied themselves with their sticks and advanced with deliberate steps.

By the time they reached the mountain path the morning sunlight was spreading over part of the sea. Eventually the line of people disappeared into the trees, past the last patches of snow on the trail.

They reappeared off the mountain trail seven days later in the early afternoon. Isaku rushed toward the path with the others. The line of people seemed to notice them and stopped. They put down their load and spread themselves along the path, sitting down or lying flat on their backs. Isaku ran over to his mother. There were bloodstains on her shoulders, and her feet were caked with dirt and blood from burst blisters. Her lips were dry, and her chest was heaving. Isaku and the other villagers used bucket yokes to carry the bales of grain from there. His mother stood up and made her way falteringly down the slope.

The straw bales of grain were stacked up in the yard at the village chief's house. Isaku's mother and the others dragged their sticks wearily into the house and sat down, their legs folded formally underneath them.

Isaku was standing in the yard, but judging from the atmosphere in the house he sensed that something was amiss. With frightened looks on their faces, every one of the people inside seemed to be clamoring to report something to the village chief. The village chief's face turned pale.

Before long the news spread that when the people selling salt had visited the labor contractor, who also doubled as a salt merchant, they had been questioned by two men. These men were from a shipping agency in a port at the southern tip of the island that ran ships on the western circuit; they had come to inquire about a twelve-hundred-bale ship that was missing. The ship was fully laden with rice and pottery, and had set sail at the end of the previous year with favorable winds behind her. It seemed that the weather had turned foul along the way, but the people at the shipping agency had not been particularly worried, because the ship's captain was a veteran sailor who had weathered many a storm in the past. But they did mention that the previous spring the ship had undergone large-scale repairs, with rotten timbers, rusty metal fittings, and such being replaced. She was an aging vessel known as the Old Granny, thirteen years past being put into commission.

The ship would have been heading north along the west coast of the island, but disappeared along the way. It failed to reach its destination, and there were also no signs of its having taken shelter in any other port. The ship's captain was an honest man; it was unthinkable that he would have made off in the ship in order to steal the cargo. Either it had been blown far out to sea, where it sank, or it had been smashed to pieces on the coast.

If the ship had been wrecked along the coast, it should be possible to retrieve part of the cargo. Because they assumed that their search should be limited to the western coastline, this was where the shipping agency had dispatched their men.

The timing of this ship's disappearance more or less matched the appearance of *O-fune-sama*, but since the vessel that rode up on the reef in front of the village had a capacity of around three hundred bales, it was clear that these men were searching for a different ship. Of course, even if the ships were different, the fact that these men were looking for a missing ship put the village in terrible jeopardy.

Isaku and the others looked anxious as they jostled their way into the dirt floor area and stared at the village chief's face.

The chief moved back to the fireplace and talked quietly with the more senior members of the community. There was still evidence in the village of all sorts of things brought to them by *O-fune-sama*. While the ship's timber had been carried away into the forest, the rice and other commodities from the cargo had been distributed among the families. If these men had someone guide them to the village and took a look inside the houses, they would find things that people of their station in life would not normally have, and would become suspicious. No doubt they would judge that the villagers had indeed plundered cargo from a wrecked ship.

The bailiffs would come to arrest the villagers and subject

them to harsh interrogation. In the course of such questioning, the village's age-old practice of luring O-fune-sama would
be revealed. If this came to pass, the village chief and many
others, including women and children, would be doomed to
a ghastly end. The village would cease to exist. The fact that
the men from the shipping agency had come as far as the
next village, and had gone out of their way to question those
selling salt, was sure proof that their village was one of the
areas where they presumed the ship might have run aground.

All of the men in council with the village chief had
turned a shade of gray; some were using both hands to stop
their knees from shaking violently. Isaku himself suddenly
started to tremble.

The slightly built village chief uttered something to the
elder, who nodded, got to his feet, and walked over to the
assembled villagers.

"Listen carefully. We're going to hide every last thing up
in the mountains. Everything O-fune-sama bestowed upon us.
You'll build huts up there to store the things in, but first of
all we must get everything into the forest. The huts'll be built
afterward," said the old man in a hollow voice.

The villagers bowed, stood up, and scurried to their
houses.

Isaku watched his mother wearily get to her feet, and he
followed behind her as she shuffled along, supporting herself
on her stick. When he thought of his mother's gashed shoulders and feet, and how she had doggedly carried all those bales
of rice, he felt miserable about his own lack of strength.

When his mother stepped inside their house, she stooped
over one of the bales of rice stacked on the dirt floor and
lifted it onto her shoulder. The heavy weight was obviously
a struggle for her as she staggered out the back door. Isaku

followed, carrying the jug of rapeseed oil and a tub of soy sauce.

His mother plodded slowly up the narrow path into the mountains behind the village. Occasionally she paused to catch her breath. Isaku looked on fearfully, worrying that his mother's back might break.

Trees stretched all around as his mother stepped off the path into the forest. Sunlight slipped through the gaps in the forest canopy, allowing peach trees to blossom in the smallest of open spaces. His mother lay the bale of rice behind a large rock and sat down, panting for breath as the sweat dripped from her brow.

"Cut some wood with the axe and make a foundation," she said, getting to her feet and heading back toward the path.

Isaku returned home and grabbed a tub full of wine, his axe, and a hatchet before going back into the forest. He sank the blade of his axe into the trunk of a tree; after felling it he trimmed off the branches with his hatchet and laid it down behind the rock. When he had several such trees lined up side by side, his mother placed the bales of straw on top. It was almost evening by the time they had stacked the eighth and last bale, part of which had already been used, and Isaku covered them with a straw raincoat and some matting.

That night his mother broke out in a terrible fever. Isaku applied a poultice of medicinal herbs to the cracked skin on her shoulders and feet, but pus oozed from the wounds. His mother clenched her teeth and groaned in pain.

The next morning Isaku made some vegetable porridge and fed his prostrate mother, as well as his younger brother and sister, before going into the forest with Isokichi. They worked hard putting together a makeshift hut from pieces of wood. Their only concern was to keep the rain and dew off the bales of rice, so they attached a grass thatch roof to the planks at the bottom. Shadows of branches swayed on the rooftop.

When they got back home, their mother was sitting by the fire roasting beans.

"Is it all right for you to be up?" Isaku asked, but his mother remained silent. Her face looked pallid and sickly, her cheeks sunken, and her splayed legs blue and swollen.

He moved the poultice of medicinal herbs from the corner of the earthen floor area next to his mother.

"Go to the chief's house and let him know that every grain of rice has been carried into the forest and that you've built a hut over it," said his mother as she continued to roast the beans.

Isaku nodded and left the house. The western sky glowed bright red, and the sea shimmered below. The color of the sky reminded him of the blood of the murdered deckhands. He hurried along the village path.

An eerie silence reigned over the village. At this time of year there was much to be gathered on the shore, but there was not a soul to be seen on the beach. Even the children sensed the mood of the adults, and they were not out playing on the village path. After hiding all the rice and other plundered goods in the mountains, the villagers spent their days cooped up indoors, holding their breath. Isaku's mother tended her wounds as she dried the grain from the other village or wove cloth on her loom.

Isaku spent his time repairing his fishing tackle, occasionally looking out the back door up the path to the next village, or out at the sea. If the men from the shipping agency were to come, it would be either along the mountain pass or by ship along the coast. There was talk of placing lookouts near the pass and on the promontories, but this was overruled because, as some people pointed out, if the lookouts were noticed, they would invite suspicion.

Isaku overheard the men of the village discussing how punishment might be carried out. He was terrified. They talked of people being whipped, then dragged around by a rope before being crucified upside down and stuck with a spear until their entrails hung out. Of people being hacked with a saw before being crucified. If it were found out that they had plundered a ship's cargo and beaten its captain to death, no doubt they would be subjected to a similar fate.

Only one path led out of the village, and to get to the next, one had to follow the narrowest of trails chiseled through the heart of the mountains, traversing a number of valleys and peaks along the way. Isaku had gone to the next village for the first time when he saw his father off into indentured service, and the overpowering impression he had come back with was enough to make him dizzy. Rows of houses, and shops selling all sorts of goods, as well as two-story buildings to accommodate travelers. The streets were crowded with people, and things that he had only heard about but had never seen, such as oxen, passed in front of him with packages lashed to their backs. In the port he had seen cargo ships as well as fishing boats. He hadn't stopped moving for a second, but cast his eyes about restlessly until he was exhausted.

They had stayed only one night in the dirt floor area of the broker's house, but Isaku would never forget the feeling of sublime tranquillity he'd experienced when they came back over the mountain pass and saw the houses below. He was sure that he could never live anywhere other than his own village.

From the moment he heard that the shipping agents were searching for a missing ship, the next village represented to Isaku all that was mysterious and frightening. The next village was part of the same island, and it belonged to the vast land across the sea. Each village had its own set of edicts, passed down through the ages.

Rare though it might be, the coming of O-fune-sama was looked upon in the same light as unexpected schools of fish appearing near the shore, or unusually large quantities of mushrooms or mountain vegetables found in the forest. O-fune-sama was part of the bounty offered by the sea, and its deliverance just barely saved the people in the village from starvation. For Isaku's village the shipwrecking of O-fune-sama was the happiest event imaginable, but for those in other places, such as the next village, it was an evil deed worthy of the supreme penalty. But if O-fune-sama had never graced their shores, the village would have long ceased to exist, and the bay would have been nothing more than an expanse of sea girded by a stretch of rocks. Their ancestors had lived there, and they themselves were able to continue on thanks only to O-fune-sama.

It was said that dead souls from their village would go far away across the sea and, in time, return to find a host among the pregnant women. There was nowhere for them to return to but their own village. If they came back to a place where the rules were different, where happy events were regarded as crimes, the result could be nothing but confusion. If Isaku were to have his own family, he knew that he would have to go to the next village to sell salt and the like, but he was determined to avoid such journeys. He wanted to stay safe in the village where fixed tenets of living were followed.

At times he thought about his own death. His body being burned and his bones buried in the ground, his soul leaving the village and heading across the water. A long journey before he reached the place far across the sea where the souls of other dead villagers would be waiting. The spirits had a settlement at the bottom of the sea where everything was bright and clear. Dense clumps of fresh green seaweed swaying like groves of trees, and all sorts of barnacles and other colorful shellfish clinging to the rocks, shining like mother-of-pearl.

Schools of little fish, silver scales glistening as they swam, turning in unison as their leader changed direction, just like a flutter of snowflakes dancing in the air.

The sea bottom was always calm and the water temperature unchanging. The dead souls looked like jellyfish in their translucent clothes, and they had a healthy sheen to their hair. They always smiled and they never talked. They were in the state of deep serenity that death brings. There he saw his grandmother, of whom he had only hazy memories, and Teru, his little sister who had died two years ago. The people standing behind them must be his ancestors.

He moved over to them and stood beside Teru. Before he knew it, he, too, was draped in translucent clothes and his face wore a gentle smile. He felt pleasantly warm inside.

At times, some spirits would drift away, seen off by those who stayed behind. They were the souls returning to the village to be reincarnated in the womb through the sexual union of man and woman. And when would reincarnation happen? Most likely a very long time after death.

He harbored no doubts that he, too, had been a reincarnated spirit in his mother's womb. He believed that the settlement of dead souls far across the sea was not just his imagining but existed so clearly in his memory because it was a place he had at one time been part of.

He had no fear of dying, especially since he believed that

there was a place to live peacefully after death. But if he were hauled away and killed in an unfamiliar place, he thought it unlikely that his spirit would reach the sanctuary for the dead souls from his village. No doubt his spirit would be doomed to a hell full of the souls of grim-faced strangers.

If the men from the shipping agency were to come to the village and find that the villagers had plundered cargo from a wrecked ship, they would be arrested and killed, they would be unable to savor the tranquillity after death. Isaku prayed that the men from the shipping agency would never appear.

The snow had started to melt in the mountains, and the houses shuddered each time the rumbling avalanches reverberated through the village. The flow of water through the small stream that ran between the houses increased to a torrent.

By March the snow had all but disappeared from the mountains; the traces glistened only on the far-off ridges. No people were to be seen on the mountain path, and no boats out on the water.

The chief summoned the more senior members of the community; it was decided that two men would be sent to the neighboring village. Their mission was to find out what the shipping agencies were doing, whether or not their village was under suspicion.

The next morning, just as if they were going to do some trading, the men shouldered bales full of dried fish and set off up the mountain path. Each had a pair of sturdy legs, and in no time they disappeared into the forest.

Five days later, around sunset, the men reappeared and hurried down to the village chief's house. Isaku joined the other villagers in front of the house.

The news the men brought put the village at ease. At the

salt merchant's where they traded the dried fish for grain, they had inquired in passing about the shipping agent's men who had stayed at the merchant's house. These men, they were told, had already returned to the shipping merchant's office at a port on the southern part of the island. They had asked the captains of ships that came into port and visitors from villages along the coast about the missing ship, but had received no clues as to what had happened.

"It must've got blown out to sea in a storm and sunk. Those fellows gave up and finally went home," the merchant had said indifferently.

The villagers exchanged delighted looks. The danger was over. However, the chief did not give them permission to carry the rice back home from the forest. They should continue to be vigilant, he decided, just in case.

In the middle of March, the ritual to pray for a good fishing catch was held on the beach, and that day the village chief gave them permission to retrieve their rice from the mountains. That night, the villagers cooked rice for their dinners, as in Isaku's family, where they boiled up a rice gruel. Isaku also had a little wine with his mother.

The next day he went out on the water in his boat with Isokichi. At first they could catch nothing but small fry. Once they were into April, however, they began to hook large sardines in great quantities. They couldn't fish together because the lines would get tangled, so Isaku entrusted the steering to Isokichi and he concentrated on catching sardines. Of course, with Isokichi still inexperienced, whenever they came near the reef Isaku would take the oar and work the boat away from the rocks. The skin on Isokichi's hands split and blood oozed out.

The sardine run seemed larger than normal, and even

from the boat they could see a teeming mass of shimmering, silvery scales darting about under the water. The color of the sea would change where they were densest, and at times whole areas of water would appear to be boiling. If he attached several hooks to his line and dropped it over the side, he felt the line being pulled right away. With sardines on almost all of the hooks, it became a chore to remove them.

In the evening when they went in to shore, they would transfer the sardines into tubs and carry them back home, where his mother would skewer them and grill them by the fire. The fish were at their succulent best, and each time some fat dripped into the fire the flames would flare up. To Isaku the taste of the hot sardines was delicious beyond compare.

His mother split some of the fish in half and got his little sister Kane to hand them to her as she hung them out on a length of twine to dry.

The temperature rose and the mountains were blanketed in greenery.

The men of the village all put their boats out at the same time, but in a slightly different way from the previous year. Normally they would go out at dawn, but some boats could be seen leaving the shore well after the sea was flooded with sunlight. They finished earlier, too, hurrying back around the time the sun started to set. There were men who used physical ailments as excuses not to put their boats out at all.

"Getting slack is the worst thing that can happen to a person," his mother muttered as she added some more wood to the fire.

The men who were no longer taking fishing seriously had been spoiled by the food brought by O-fune-sama. They would use all they caught to feed their families and saw no need for additional catch to barter for grain. Fortunately, this year sardines had come in force, and one could bring in a large catch without having to spend too much time out on the water. They could even take days off.

Isaku wanted to take it easy, too, but when he thought of what his mother had said, he could not bring himself to do so.

The sea was calm for days on end and occasionally it drizzled from morning to night. Even on such days Isaku would take Isokichi out in the boat. His mother tilled their little field and planted vegetable seeds. From out on the water he could see the terraced fields carved out of the hillside, and he often watched the sedge hats moving in the field worked by Tami's family.

One day in mid-April, a man in a boat near Isaku called to him across the water and pointed to the mountain path. Isaku felt a chill run up his spine. He could see what appeared to be two men, walking slowly toward the village. They were a long way away and difficult to make out properly, but it seemed as if they were looking at Isaku. He thought they must be the men from the shipping agency. He had heard that they had stopped their search for the ship and gone home, but maybe they had not given up but had simply gone to another village before heading here. Bales of rice and other exotic bounty from O-fune-sama were back in the village; if the agents spotted it, they would know that it had been plundered from a ship.

Isaku began to shake all over.

He looked back at the boat next to his. The man was staring at Isaku. He turned his eyes to the mountain but lost sight of the two men as they disappeared behind the trees along the sides of the path.

Isaku followed the other boats as they turned back toward

shore, relieving Isokichi of the oar and rowing with all his might. No time to move the bales of rice back up into the forest, but he thought at least he could try to hide them by throwing some matting on top.

Boats were reaching the shore one after another as Isaku pulled his out of the water and onto the sand before running back to his house. The women and children, who would normally be down near the water's edge, had already disappeared.

Isaku ran into their house to find his mother covering the bales of rice with straw matting and stacking firewood on top. He helped her carry the jars and tubs of wine, white sugar, and soy sauce out the back door and hide them in a bamboo grove.

He peeked from behind their house toward the mountain path. The treetops were swaying in the wind as the sun beat down. Only the sound of the waves was heard as a profound stillness spread through the village. Every one of the villagers cowered indoors.

He could see movement between the tree trunks, and before long the two men appeared at the top of the path. One of them was supporting himself with a long stick, the other was helping him down the path. The man with the stick had had one leg cut off at the knee.

These men certainly didn't look anything like Isaku's idea of people from a shipping agency. Surely they wouldn't send a crippled man on a job of this kind. Besides, they were poor, their clothes little better than rags.

The two men came to a halt a short way down the path, alternately staring at the village and casting their eyes out to sea, before crumpling to their knees on the ground, sobbing.

Isaku's mother stepped out and walked in their direction. Isaku followed her as men and women began to emerge from their houses and head up toward the mountain path. The wariness he had felt earlier had all but dissolved when he saw a woman run ahead of the crowd and embrace the man with the stick.

"Someone's back from bondage," said his mother, quickening her step.

Isaku's father had another year left before his term was up, so it wasn't him. Isaku followed his mother and the other villagers. The two men were now sitting on the ground, their faces a dark reddish in color, their cheeks sunken and hollow. Isaku recognized neither of them, both men seemingly in their forties, one completely gray, the other almost bald.

They had returned after finishing their ten-year indentures. The villagers were surprised to see how much the two had aged, obviously an indication of how hard they had been worked. The man with the stick had gone into the forest to fell trees in deep snow and had fallen from a cliff when hauling the timber out. He was knocked unconscious and saved only because the other men had searched for him. They had found him two days later, buried up to his waist in snow. While the other injuries he received in the fall had healed, his left foot, which had been under the snow, had turned gangrenous. Because this could lead to death, they had amputated his leg at the knee. Crippled as he was, he was indeed fortunate to have got back to the village alive.

Isaku's father was bonded in the same port as these two men, so that evening his mother went to ask how her husband was faring.

She came back after about an hour, poured herself a cup of wine, and sat down near the fire.

Isaku thought something was wrong when he saw his mother's worried expression. Maybe the men had brought bad news about Isaku's father. Perhaps his father was already dead. Nervously he moved toward his mother as she started to sip her wine.

"Did he say anything about Father?"

"That he's well . . . ," muttered his mother, her eyes fixed on the flames. Isaku felt greatly relieved and sat himself down by the fire.

"They said he works so hard that the shipping agency people have their eyes on him. Said your father's a strong man, he encourages other villagers, helps them along. But they said your father's worried about us, hopes we're all well. . . ." His mother took a gulp of wine.

She must be thinking about Teru. Thinking that she had let little Teru die and feeling that she had let their father down. She must be feeling miserable over her own powerlessness. The wine was her way of drowning her sorrows.

Isaku sat silently, staring into the flames. He imagined Teru, far away across the sea, standing under the water, dressed in translucent clothes, a gentle smile on her face. Teru's death had been beyond his mother's power to stop, and her short time on this earth must have been what her life span was destined to be. Yes, she might have died, but being surrounded by the spirits of their ancestors meant that she was not alone as she rested peacefully out there at the bottom of the sea.

"Father'll be back next spring. We've just got to hold out a little longer," Isaku said as he put another piece of wood on the fire.

His mother said nothing, slowly handing the cup of wine to Isaku. He felt emotion welling up inside him. This was the first time his mother had shown him any affection since his father had gone into bondage. Isaku sensed that his mother now recognized him as someone she could depend on.

He took a sip of the wine and passed the cup back to his mother.

Isokichi muttered something in his sleep as he rolled over. The cup still in her hand, his mother sat staring at Isokichi's face looming pale in the light of the fire.

The sardine season was over, and they started to catch squid. Each household was busy cutting and hanging squid out to dry. The idleness that had infected the community since they had been blessed with bounties from O-fune-sama gradually faded away, and the change in seasons seemed to have brought with it a return to normal routine.

On calm days a string of boats would put out onto the water early in the morning, and women and children could be seen on the shore looking for shellfish or seaweed. On days when the sea was high, Isaku would spend his time working on his boat. One of the men who had returned from servitude came down to the beach, sat on the sand with his stick at his side, and cast his eyes out to sea. Isaku stopped working and walked over to squat beside the man, whose face brightened when Isaku mentioned his father's name. "You say my father's doing all right, then . . . ," said Isaku, looking questioningly at the man.

"He's fine. Your father's made of steel, he never even catches a cold."

Isaku nodded in reply. "I suppose the work must be pretty hard."

"That it is, my boy. Bond slaves are bought by the masters, you know. They can do what they like with you. The only thing they're afraid of is that we'll die on 'em and they'll lose their money, so they give you plenty to eat."

A grimace realigned the wrinkles on the man's face as he recalled the hardships of the work in the port.

"My dad must worry about us all here."

"The only time I heard him say anything about you was when we left the port to come back here. Otherwise he didn't talk about his family. I guess he thinks that kind of family talk would make the others feel bad. He's doing a real good job looking after the others."

The man looked out to sea, his gray hair ruffled by the wind as sand blew up onto what remained of his leg. Ten years as a bond slave had taken its toll.

"Just glad to have come back after O-fune-sama. I've had some rice, some wine, and even a puff on some tobacco. The village chief told me to take it easy for a while, but as soon as I feel a bit better I want to get out on the water," said the man with a joyful glint in his eye.

Isaku mused at how happy his father would be if he knew that the village had been blessed by a visit from O-fune-sama. Indeed, not only his father but all of the bond slaves would be glad to know that the families they had left behind had been delivered from starvation.

Several days later the crippled man's companion on the journey back to the village died. His family found him one morning lying stiff and cold in his straw bedding. Whether it had been the feeling of release from his labors or he gorged himself to death, they would never know, but he must have succumbed quietly during the night.

The one-legged man's grief at the wake brought many of the villagers to tears. From the time they had set off from the port, sleeping under the stars for nights on end, until they reached the village, the younger man had looked after his crippled friend, helping him struggle over the mountain passes and through the sheer valleys. No doubt this was fixed in his mind as he clung to the dead body lashed to the funeral post, crying, "Why him, why not me?"

The next day the body was placed in a coffin and carried to the cemetery. The one-legged man made his way slowly up the hill, steadying himself with his walking stick. As the coffin was engulfed in flames, he crouched down and wept in front of the pyre.

The villagers went into mourning, but some found comfort in the thought that the man had died in his own village. Many bond servants died away from home; this man had been fortunate enough to at least set foot in the village again and enjoy some time with his family.

As the green mantle around the village deepened in color and the sun's rays grew stronger by the day, flies swarmed on the lines of dried squid. As was the custom every year, the women headed for the neighboring village to sell the squid, and Isaku's mother joined them. Two of the village elders accompanied the women to sound out whether their village was still the object of suspicion, but on their return they reported to the chief that they had seen nothing unusual.

A tranquil mood came over the village. Occasionally ships sailed by, but the villagers were no longer worried and merely watched them fade into the distance.

As the squid catch started to fall away, the rainy season came, at times with heavy cloudbursts. One day when the sea was rough, Isaku set off early in the morning with Isokichi into the forest behind the village. The sun shone through a slit in the otherwise thickly clouded sky, casting a swath of bright sunlight on the mountain path. Once they got deeper into the forest they started stripping the bark from linden trees. As there had been no cloth on board *O-fune-sama*, all the families in the village were resorting to collecting bark.

Isaku's mother had finished making a jacket for his father by early spring of that year, and now it seemed she wanted to make something for the children.

Isaku bundled up most of the bark and lashed it to his own carrying frame before loading the rest onto Isokichi's back. They stepped out of the forest and headed down the mountain path. The twittering of birds filled the air, and high above them they could hear the song of a nightingale. The sun was still on the ascent, so Isaku felt satisfied that, with Isokichi's help, he had managed to finish earlier than expected.

Feeling thirsty, he thought they should take a rest on the bank of a nearby stream. He called out to Isokichi as he set his load on the path and made his way down the slope, stepping from rock to rock. Before long they heard the sound of swiftly flowing water and saw the stream itself glistening through the trees.

Isaku stopped. He noticed someone by the water's edge. Isokichi had noticed, too, and was peering between the trees. Two people were squatting on the bank facing the stream, a girl with her hair tied up in a knot and next to her a little boy. Isaku felt himself flush. From the look of the girl, it could only be Tami. Isaku could hardly turn back, so he headed down the slope. Tami turned around, as did the little boy; Isaku recognized him as Tami's four-year-old brother. Seeing the distrustful look in the girl's eyes, Isaku forced a smile as he approached. Tami's little brother smiled back, but Tami's steely glare was unchanged. There were two baskets on the ground beside them, full of the slender bamboo shoots they had collected.

Isaku squatted down by the stream a short distance away and scooped some water up to his mouth. He was so preoccupied with Tami's presence that the water didn't feel cold at all. Isokichi walked over to Tami and her brother and talked with them. Isaku wet the cloth he had hanging from his belt and wiped the sweat from his brow.

"She's ripped a toenail off," said Isokichi. Isaku looked at Tami and saw her trying to cool one foot by dipping it in the stream. He ran back up the slope; in a flat area to the left of the path he saw some bushes; he had been there before with his father collecting *otogirisō*, and he stepped between the bushes, picking leaves as he went. Scampering back to the stream, Isaku handed the herb to Isokichi. "Tell her to rub this between her hands," he said, "then into the wound. It'll stop the bleeding." Isokichi nodded and took it to Tami. She glanced at Isaku but turned her attention at once to the *otogirisō*, rubbing it together in her hands, then applying it to her toe. Isaku had looked away.

He kept his eyes firmly fixed on the flow of the water, but at the same time he was keenly aware that Tami and her brother were making their way up the slope.

Isokichi drank some water from his cupped hands, then sat on a rock and dipped his feet into the stream. Isaku wet the cloth once more and roughly washed his face.

That night Isaku lay wide awake in his bed. He kept thinking of his chance meeting with Tami, how he had given her the *otogirisō* to stop her foot bleeding, and wondered how she had felt. That she had rubbed the herb on the wound must mean that she had accepted his gesture as well meant. That was enough for him. If they had happened to meet with no one else around, in all likelihood she would have taken fright and run away. He thought how each of them having their younger brother with them had provided him with the opportunity to show goodwill toward Tami. Indeed, she had been receptive to his kindness.

Isaku had noticed how Tami's figure was becoming increasingly feminine. Although he was only a year younger, Tami seemed to be maturing at a faster rate. He had dreams of making her his wife, but held little hope of realizing them. His eyes glistened wide open in the dark as he sighed again and again.

With the rain showing no signs of abating, the inside of the house felt increasingly damp. His mother made the most of sunny spells and spread their supplies of grain and fish out on a straw mat to dry.

One evening when Isaku returned home, his mother pointed to a new sedge hat lying on the floor. "Tami brought it for you. She said it's for something you did for her." Isaku stared at the hat. No doubt it was for the help he had given her by the stream. He felt himself flushing red at the thought that Tami was grateful to him.

Embarrassed that his mother might see his blushing face, Isaku put down his fishing tackle in the corner of the dirt floor and slipped out the back door. Once outside he stepped over to the tiny stream behind their house and washed his hands and feet. He mused that in that short time up in the mountains, Tami must have noticed that his hat was battered and torn. Normally the villagers made sedge hats indoors when the snow was thick on the ground, but Tami must have made this one since they had met by the stream.

Without questioning Isaku as to why Tami should be giving him such a gift, his mother busied herself sorting the linden bark, boiling the inner layers and putting it to soak in a stream of water flowing down from the hills. Turning her spinning wheel, she transformed it into thread, then sat herself down in front of the loom.

The sedge hat didn't move from where it had been hung on the wooden post. Isaku wanted very much to wear it, but the prospect of attracting his mother's attention held him back. Not only that, to Isaku this was no ordinary hat, but a hat too precious to expose to the elements.

But the light rain on the first day of the saury season was enough for him to muster the courage to grab the hat, securing it firmly on his head by tying the strings under his chin. He felt exhilarated at the thought that he was wearing a hat that Tami had made with her own hands.

He stopped the boat and dropped the anchor when he got to Crow Point. First he draped a straw mat over the side, then he let another drift out from the stern. Isokichi was all eyes as he studied what was to him a brand-new way of fishing.

The two of them pressed themselves low as they watched the straw matting drift behind the boat. By the end of the previous year's season, Isaku had more or less mastered grabbing the fish with his hands, but now he felt anything but confident that he still had the knack, and the last thing he wanted was to be shamed in front of his younger brother. For ten days the best he could do was grab two or three fish a day, and some days he couldn't even get one. But gradually his catch increased, and before very long he was bringing home more than a dozen fish a day.

On several occasions, in the evening, Isaku had caught sight of Tami carrying a catch of saury home. Tami's father was known for his skill in making dugouts, but he was also quite a fisherman and would routinely bring in large catches of saury for his family. Tami would fill two wooden pails with saury and carry them off the beach suspended on either end of a carrying rod. Occasionally their eyes would meet, but she would quickly avert her gaze; her expression gave nothing away.

With the start of the rainy season, the summer heat intensified. The sun turned Isokichi's skin a dark shade of
brown, and the sea breezes made his hair dry. About the time
their mother finished preparing two big wooden tubs of salted
saury, the catch suddenly fell away. A poor season in comparison with the previous year, the villagers said.

The Bon festival was a more lively celebration than usual.
Rice was served in all the houses; they even put offerings of
little rice balls on their family altars. But in Isaku's house, it
was rice gruel, with some boiled seaweed to go with it.

Blistering-hot days continued, and at times there were
thunderstorms, engulfing the village in a white mist as the
skies opened wide. After the squid started biting again, Isaku
spent his days on the water with Isokichi. At times he would
look at the line of mountains towering above the village. The
midsummer sun beat down on the leaves of the trees, creating
a deep green cloak of vibrant color. The narrow path carved into
the face of the mountain disappeared into the trees. Isaku's
heart raced at the thought that he would see his father come
down that path the following spring. They said his father was
fit and well; no doubt he would come down the path prac-
tically running. He would grieve over Teru's death, but he
would not blame Isaku's mother. He might even be relieved
to hear that Teru was the only one. His father was passing
his days without any word of his family. How happy he would
be if he knew that they had been blessed with a visit by
O-fune-sama.

"Wonder if O-fune-sama'll come again this winter," said
Isokichi as he worked the oar.

"Maybe she will, or maybe we won't see her again for a
few years yet," replied Isaku as he stopped jiggling the cloth-
baited spear in the water and turned his eyes toward Crow

Point. He could picture the scene he had looked down on from the top of the promontory: the villagers in little boats converging on the wrecked ship, ferrying the cargo to the shore and dismantling the hull. It had been a bustling scene, played out at a brisk pace. Isaku wondered whether his brother would be right and this winter would see such a scene repeated, or whether he would never set eyes on *O-fune-sama* again as long as he lived.

Above the point crows circled in the sky. Like little black dots.

7

As summer came to an end the vil-
lage was lashed by one squall after another. One day, starting
around noon, a warm, damp wind rose and black clouds sped
across the sky. The rain began as large, distinct drops, but
before long increased in intensity until veritable torrents of
water were pouring from the heavens. As dusk came and went
the tempest redoubled in strength. Rain pelted the wooden
walls and thatched roof. Inside, Isaku and Isokichi propped a
board against the straw mat in the doorway and tied the mat
over the window in place with twine.

Isaku huddled in his straw bedding, but his sleep was dis-
turbed as the wind gusting down from the mountains dashed
pieces of broken branches and leaves noisily against the roof.
As the house shuddered, and at times felt as if it was being
lifted off the ground, Isaku was afraid that the wind would
blow the roof off.

The next morning the wind was still strong, but the rain
had stopped. The ground was covered with broken branches,

and a sea of leaves mixed with dirt washed down the slope. The sky had cleared by noon, but the waves were still high and each line of crashing breakers glistened in the bright sunlight. The signs of autumn became more pronounced with each passing day. The squid catch swelled as the sea grew calm.

Isaku's mother worked hard cutting and hanging up squid to dry, but she still found time to pick wild vegetables in the mountains behind the village. She put bamboo shoots in their vegetable porridge and fed them dry roasted buds picked off the runners of yams she had found up in the forest. Isaku looked forward to mealtimes because this season provided them with the widest selection of food in the year.

And yet his mother looked thoroughly dejected. Though they used the rice sparingly in gruel, they had already eaten their way through one of the straw bales and were now on the second. At times she would scoop up some rice with a bowl, only to pause in thought before pouring it back into the bale. Once this and the remaining six full bales were finished, they would again be faced with the prospect of starvation. For Isaku, too, the thought was frightening.

His mother went up to their little patch of dirt carved out of the hillside and came back with a bag holding what little grain had survived long enough to ripen. Sitting in a corner of the room, she ground this into flour with a stone mortar. The next day she joined the women going to the next village. Each carried on her back a load of dried squid to barter for beans. There was a look of foreboding in her eyes with winter looming and, with it, the prospect of gathering no more food.

Around the time the ears began to appear on the eulalia grass, the men started to go out after octopus, and the village became decidedly more animated. Isaku took Isokichi out with him and taught his brother how to catch octopus using a barbed fishing spear.

Isokichi finally mastered the oar, and, cautious by nature, if he sensed they were getting too close to the reef, he quickly turned the little boat away to a safe distance. The younger boy was growing fast, and it was clear that by the time he matured he would surpass his brother in physical size. He followed his elder brother's instructions without question, and he learned quickly. There was no doubt that Isaku admired his little brother and loved him dearly.

Their mother called Isokichi "Iso." Before he started fishing, she used this diminutive as though she were talking to a young child, but more recently her tone implied that she now took her younger son seriously as a worker. Isokichi might have been a boy of few words, but he certainly applied himself diligently to his assigned tasks.

The temperature dropped by the day, and out of nowhere red dragonflies appeared in incredible numbers: droves of them flew through the air or alighted to rest their wings. There seemed to be many more of them than in previous years. The octopus started to leave the shore, and the eulalia ears dried up and were blown away by the wind.

When the sea turned rough, Isaku and Isokichi headed into the mountains to gather firewood, enough to take them through the winter. As they made their way along the mountain path, Isaku looked around in the hope that he might meet Tami, and though they passed other villagers on the trail, they never once saw her. Maybe she was at home weaving cloth from linden bark, he thought, or maybe she was busy making something useful out of bamboo.

One day Isaku thought they would go off the trail and

down to the stream. Sitting by the bank they found Sahei beside a pack frame loaded high with bundles of firewood. Sahei turned around, the bristles on his upper lip and chin giving him a decidedly adult look.

Isaku drank water from the stream and sat down on a rock next to Sahei. Red dragonflies buzzed past his head.

"No more fish this year," said Sahei, turning to Isaku.

Isaku nodded. The octopus had been just as scarce as the previous year, and had all but disappeared by now. This year's trade with the next village wouldn't bring them much grain.

"How much of your rice have you gone through?" asked Sahei inquiringly.

"We're on our second bale. And that's down to about two-thirds' full," said Isaku dolefully.

"That all? You must be really going easy. We're onto our fourth bale, and that's already half gone. Grandfather's to blame. He could die any day, but he asks us to keep feeding him. Legs are all swollen and he's wasting away, but he's still selfish," Sahei said, frowning.

Isaku listened apprehensively. Sahei's family must have been given at least ten bales of rice; at the rate they were going, their supply would probably last only another three years. Getting used to the taste of rice could only lead to more being consumed, bringing the day it would run out even closer.

"Not just us either. There's quite a few who've already gone through more than half their store. Not many families around who're only on their second bale," said Sahei enviously.

Isaku thought of his mother's frugality. The only times she cooked rice for them were at New Year and the Bon festival when she would place some before the family's altar. Even then it would be as gruel, with water added for good measure. No doubt her prudence stemmed from her fierce determination to see the rest of her children survive even though their father was away.

"Hope O-fune-sama comes again this year," murmured Sahei.

"They say she often comes two years in a row," Isaku offered, appraising Sahei's expression from the side.

"So they say," Sahei agreed, nodding. The two of them sat there for a while, gazing into the water. Sahei got to his feet and shouldered his pack-frame load of firewood. Isaku and Isokichi did the same, moving away from the stream up the slope and back to the path.

By the time the village was enveloped in autumn colors, the red dragonflies had disappeared. With the sea turning colder by the day, the catch was reduced to small fry.

The person chosen to act as that year's pregnant woman in the ritual ceremony for O-fune-sama was a slightly built girl of sixteen. She threw the straw festoon into the sea and overturned the table in the village chief's house. But it was a weak performance in comparison with the previous year's, the food in the bowl barely spilling on the floor.

The leaves on the trees turned from red to yellow and fell to the ground, but still no fires were lit on the beach. The sea was unusually calm for this time of year, so there was little point in lighting the fires under the cauldrons.

Isaku put his boat out on the water every day, occasionally catching a large fish, almost a foot long, that he had never set eyes on before. This was a bony fish called gin, which was said to appear in early winter once or twice every ten years. True to its name, it was a brilliant silver. The older fishermen thought it strange that not only were there so many calm days but also that gin should be appearing.

No sooner did the leaves stop falling than the village had

its first snow of the winter. At first it was little more than a flurry, but as night fell it became heavier, and by the next day it was a violent storm. The sea finally moved with the change of season, and the sound of the breakers pounding the shore assaulted the village.

The snow stopped after three days, leaving the village covered in a white sheet. That night the fires were lit under the salt cauldrons. Folklore had it that the winter sea would be rough for four days, then calm for the next two, and indeed this proved to be the case. On the calm days Isaku put his boat out on the water and again caught nothing but *gin*. It was a thin-fleshed fish with a bland taste. Rather than grilled, it was best tenderized with a knife to break up the little bones, and then either eaten raw or used to make dumplings for soup.

When Isaku's turn on the cauldrons came, he kept the fires blazing from dusk to dawn. As he sat in the little hut warming himself by the fire, he looked out into the darkness, picturing in his mind's eye the scene at the end of the previous year with *O-fune-sama* leaning to one side as she sat wrecked on the reef.

He could make out nothing more than the dull white of the waves breaking on the shore, and as he looked out into the darkness he wondered whether *O-fune-sama* might not indeed be already sitting out there hard and fast in the grip of the reef. The thought that the rice in those bales lying on the floor at home would eventually run out made him feel helpless and ill at ease. But Isaku and his family were indeed fortunate compared to Sahei's, who must surely be distressed at their situation. Getting used to the taste of rice made the prospect of life without it unbearable.

Snow fell most days, and the village was buried beneath

a thick white blanket. When the sea was rough, Isaku stayed and worked at home, mending his fishing tackle or cutting wood for the fire. Isokichi went into the woods behind their house to set traps and occasionally came back with a rabbit, which he skinned and cut up according to his mother's instructions.

At times, when Isaku was half asleep, he would suddenly sit up, imagining that he could hear shouting. He would look out the door thinking that maybe O-fune-sama had come again, but there was nothing but the sound of the waves. Shivering in the bitter cold, he would hurry back to his straw bedding.

The fires on the beach were lit without fail every night when the sea ran high, and at dawn Isaku's mother would carry the salt from the cauldrons to the village. The chill in the air was much more severe than in a normal winter, and the snow on the ground was frozen hard. Ships on the coastal run passed by within sight, while vessels from the clans plied the deeper waters farther offshore. Some, with sails trimmed, would speed past, bobbing up and down in the heavy seas.

As the year drew to an end, all the villagers' faces took on the same despondent expression because they had now entered the time of the year when no more cargo ships would be passing by their shores. Yes, some had said that in the past O-fune-sama had come in successive winters, but to Isaku that appeared to be nothing more than wishful thinking.

The year came to an end, and a new one began. Their chances of being visited by O-fune-sama had gone. Each household prepared the New Year's meal of boiled rice and grilled fish. Isaku's family was no exception, as they, too, placed their offering of rice in a bowl in front of their altar and lit a candle.

Isaku accompanied his mother and younger brother and sister through the snow to pay their respects at their ancestral graves. His mother scooped the snow away from the grave-stones, then stood for some time, palms pressed together in prayer. His mother could only be praying that his father would return safely to the village after his term of bondage ended in the spring.

They had rice again with their evening meal, this time in gruel, and as his mother sat there sipping away, she turned to look at the remaining bales stacked on the dirt floor. "Your father'll be surprised when he sees bales of rice sitting here."

After New Year there was an unseasonal spell of calm weather, but by the middle of January the heavy seas were back with a vengeance. Isaku and Isokichi spent their days either collecting shellfish and kelp washed up on the shore, or cutting firewood. Their mother was busy making straw mats or weaving on her loom.

One night at the end of January, Isaku awoke suddenly from a deep sleep. His feet felt like blocks of ice in the intense cold. Looking at the straw matting hanging over the window, he sensed that dawn was not far away. Snuggling into his straw bedding, he shut his eyes, only to open them again. He thought he could hear voices mingled with the sound of the waves. Maybe he was imagining it; but then he made out what was unmistakably the sound of someone yelling, a full-bodied roar, closer to the bellowing of an animal than of a human.

He sat bolt upright and looked around to see the rest of the family sound asleep. Getting to his feet he poked the last embers in the fire and put on a few pieces of wood. The fire sparked into life, and the light threw dark shadows about the walls. Still thinking that his senses might have been playing tricks on him, Isaku sat in front of the fire warming his hands as he strained to hear what might be going on outside.

This time he heard a strident voice, a man shouting "Oooi." Isaku flushed with excitement as he crawled over to his mother's bed and shook her awake. She raised herself on one elbow and stared bleary-eyed at Isaku. She remained motionless as she strained to make out the noises in the night, then jumped to her feet. Trying to keep up with his mother, Isokichi hurriedly threw his clothes on and pulled a straw cape over his head.

Isaku swung an axe on his shoulder, grabbed a long-bladed hoe and a hatchet, and ran out of the door behind his mother and Isokichi. The first signs of dawn were in the air, and the stars were beginning to fade. He could just make out the horizon. Voices came from the shore as Isaku, his mother, and Isokichi hurried along the path through the knee-deep snow.

He could see a boat not too far out from the shore, where a number of villagers had already gathered, some holding firebrands. The waves crashed onto the shore, throwing white spume into the air. A chant of sutras rose as the village chief arrived, accompanied by half a dozen people.

"O-fune-sama's come," said Gonsuke, who had been on duty at the salt cauldrons, his voice trembling as he knelt in front of the village chief. The chief nodded back, unable to disguise his excitement.

Suddenly a cheer erupted from the villagers, who had until then been deathly silent. Isaku couldn't believe that they were being visited by O-fune-sama two winters in a row. Maybe good things do come in twos after all, he thought.

The sky brightened and the ship was now clearly visible. She was smaller than the one that had come at the start of the previous winter and would probably carry only about a hundred bales as cargo. Her size wasn't the only thing that stood out; she was badly dilapidated and clearly not one of the sturdy clan ships.

"Quiet!" barked the elder abruptly. "Doesn't look like a shipwreck," he then said in a tone close to a whisper.

Isaku took another look at the ship, and sure enough he could see no sign of damage to the hull itself, and the rudder blade certainly seemed to be in one piece. There were no sails, just bare masts. The ship was floating in a channel in the reef, drifting gradually toward the shore. There was certainly nothing resembling cargo to be seen.

"Looks like she's just drifted in," said the man standing next to Isaku. Indeed, judging from her lack of sail, she must have just ridden the currents from farther up the coast. There didn't seem to be anyone on board, so she couldn't have been lured by the lights on the shore.

A thin veil of cloud covered the sky, but the sea was getting brighter by the minute. The villagers extinguished their flaming torches. The elder talked with the village chief for a time before addressing the villagers. "Put out the boats, check if there's any cargo on board. Be careful while you're at it, there's a swell out there," he said.

Half a dozen men hurried to the shore, pushing three little boats stern first into the water. Bobbing up and down on the turbulent sea, the boats made their way straight toward the horizon and were then skillfully turned to thread their way through the reef to the ship.

The three boats slowed and came up alongside the ship. The people standing on the shore saw one of the men jump nimbly on board the larger vessel. They could see him looking around before he disappeared from view below deck. Isaku felt uneasy. A ship that drifted in should be safe; but what if some of the crew were lying in wait to murder the unsuspecting villager, who as far as Isaku could make out had recklessly stepped down, alone and unarmed, into the bowels of the vessel?

The man eventually reappeared on deck, whence he clambered down into his boat. The three little boats pushed away from the side of the ship and headed back to shore. The village chief walked down to the water's edge, followed by the villagers.

One after another the little boats touched land, to be swiftly pulled onto the snow-covered beach.

One of the men stepped from his boat and knelt in front of the chief.

"Cargo?" asked the elder standing beside the chief.

"Almost nothing. Just three sacks of charcoal and an empty rice tray."

"Anyone on board?"

"All dead. About twenty of 'em. And they're all dressed in red. None of 'em are rotting, so they haven't been dead too long."

"All in red?" said the elder, looking skeptically at the man.

"All in red. Their clothes are red. And so are their belts and socks. And why I don't know," said the man incredulously, "but there's a red monkey mask tied to the mainmast below deck."

Snow began to fall. Isaku looked out toward the ship, which was rocking ever so slightly in the water.

"The empty rice tray could mean the people on board starved to death. But why would they put out with no cargo on board?" said the elder, tilting his head in disbelief. The only reason to risk setting sail in winter's rough seas would be to carry rice or some other important cargo. A ship's captain would sail only when satisfied that his trained eye was right about the weather. While this could end in disaster, of course, it was nevertheless part and parcel of the sailor's destiny.

Setting sail without any cargo on board was completely beyond the bounds of common sense. Besides, it was incomprehensible why each and every one of the men on the ship should be dressed in red.

"Maybe this was some kind of ceremonial ship to celebrate something," said the elder, his eyes shining as if he had finally grasped a vital clue to solving the puzzle.

"Bright red has the meaning of celebration. We dress people in bright red to celebrate old age, and I've even heard stories about people whose coffins are painted red to symbolize their lives' being brought to an appropriate end. I've seen a priest from the next village dressed in bright red, and he was a high-ranking priest, too," added the elder in a forthright tone.

Isaku had no reason to doubt the elder's interpretation. After all, in their village it was customary for a midwife to tie her sleeves up with a red cord when delivering a newborn, since the birth was a cause for celebration.

"If it's a ship that has sailed as some sort of celebration, what kind of celebration could it be?" said one of the men, looking questioningly at the elder.

"That I don't know. They had a celebration and got on board the ship all wearing red clothes. Then suddenly the weather turned rough, and they must have been blown right out to sea. They ate the little food they had, and eventually they must have died of the cold and starvation. Considering there's no cargo, that's the only thing I can think of," said the elder, looking at the village chief for support.

The villagers were silent. Several among their number nodded in agreement. The fact that this ship had not gone aground on the reef while trying to seek safe harbor meant it was different from previous O-fune-sama. All the people on board being dead must mean that it had drifted into the little village bay merely transported on the currents and blown by the winds.

Isaku supposed that the bright red clothes on the corpses were an indication of the nature of the ship itself. It reminded him of the color of the rising sun, the start of a new day, its brightness also representing the continuation of life. The bright red at dusk was reassuring, promising that as one day came to a close another would follow. Isaku thought that it was indeed fortunate for their village to have been blessed by the visit of this ship and its richly clad passengers.

"Revered elder," stammered the man who had checked below the ship's decks. The elder turned to face him.

"The bodies on the ship, they've got scars from what must have been spots. All over them. Faces, arms, legs . . . Terrible pockmarks," said the man, grimacing. The villagers looked fixedly at the two men.

"Spots?" replied the elder skeptically.

The snowfall was suddenly heavier. The elder stared out at the ship in front of them.

"There's all sorts of 'spots.' What kind of spots do you mean?" snapped the elder impatiently.

The man looked as though he was brooding over something and paused before replying. "It was dark below deck and I couldn't see all that well, but they looked like the sort of thing you get with a rash."

"If it's a rash, maybe they ate some fish that was spoiled, or even a fish that was poisonous. If they'd run out of rice and were starving, they might very well eat that kind of fish," said a man standing next to Isaku.

"But if it was just a simple rash, that wouldn't leave pock-marks. If there're pockmarks on the bodies, then it's some other sickness," retorted a middle-aged man, silencing the man beside Isaku. Another, voice trembling with cold, said, "It could be the fever-flower," at which the hint of a smile crossed the elder's face. This was the first time Isaku had heard the name of this illness, so he had no idea why the elder should find it amusing.

"The fever-flower?" said a young man, looking question-ingly at the elder. The same middle-aged man replied, "You haven't heard of it? On my trips to the next village I've seen lots of men smitten with the fever-flower. They get spots all over their face and arms and legs, and pus oozes out of those spots. The spots are shaped a bit like plum or cotton flowers, and sometimes they get a fever, so it's called the fever-flower." Turning to the man who checked below deck, he asked, "Were the spots on the bodies a reddish color? Did they look anything like the shape of a flower?"

"Now that you mention it, I've seen men in that condi-tion sitting on the side of the road in the next village, and the spots looked just like that. No, it's not a rash," he said, nodding back and forth.

Listening to the men's conversation, Isaku realized that there were many things he had yet to learn. He'd been to the next village before, but he'd never seen men with spots of that description. He wondered what on earth could cause such a hideous disease.

Several men had cleared snow away down to the sand

and were now busy lighting a fire with the sticks and firewood from the hut used as shelter during salt-making. Surrounded by the throng of villagers on the beach, the chief stood pensively in front of the flames. The elder proceeded to make an announcement: "I had thought that this boat was part of some kind of celebration. It would seem that's not the case. This must have been done as a punishment. The fever-flower is a disease that afflicts men whose lust leads them to associate with loose women. Such women carry the pox, so when a man indulges himself, the disease spreads all over his body from his private parts. The fever-flower is heaven's punishment for the lustful. No doubt the village or town chief collected those men together whose boils stank of the evil disease and put them on this ship, taking them out to sea and leaving them to drift on the currents. The fact that there are no sails or oars can only mean that they were banished, meant to drift to their deaths at the ends of the seas."

Isaku finally understood the nature of the sickness. In the next village there were houses and streets bustling with people and cattle. There were all sorts of shops, even places where you could buy food or drink if you had the money. Money, it seemed, could buy you anything. The people in the next village looked as if they were enjoying lives free from want, but at the same time this hideous disease called the fever-flower was lurking as the spoils of carnal pleasure. So that was why the elder had smiled when he mentioned the words "fever-flower."

The village chief deliberately turned to look at the elder, taking a deep breath before announcing, "Even if there is no cargo on her, there is no changing the fact that she's O-fune-sama. We've been blessed with this visit, so we can't just push her back out to sea."

The elder nodded gravely.

"That's true. But as we can see from here, she's little more than an old tub, and her timbers would be good for nothing more than firewood. There doesn't seem to be anything of value among her tools, either. Even so, let's at least get them on shore. It sounds as if the only thing we could use is the clothes on the bodies," he replied.

"And we won't get the disease if we take the clothes off these bodies?" asked the village chief, a troubled look in his narrowed eyes.

"There's no chance of that. The fever-flower is transferred only when a man penetrates a woman who is carrying the disease. Even with clothes soiled by pus or blood from the boils, if we use them after they've been washed thoroughly, there is nothing to fear," replied the elder in a tone brimming with confidence.

Seemingly satisfied, the village chief nodded in agreement.

"We only get to see things like these red clothes in the next village. They're certainly a sight. Say we keep them for young children to wear or use them at celebrations. These red clothes could very well be an omen of good fortune," said the elder. Again the village chief nodded approvingly.

Turning to the men, the elder bellowed out a command. "Well then, get out there and strip the clothes off the bodies. Claim whatever fittings you can. Then tow it out and let it drift away on the current. It'll break up and sink before too long."

The men nodded in unison, then dashed to the water's edge. Five boats were pushed out onto the water. Bobbing up and down in a line, they made their way to the ship through what was by now a fierce snowfall.

Isaku planted his axe upright in the snow and stood there mesmerized by the movements of the little boats. They drew up alongside the ship and the men disappeared below deck. In his mind's eye, Isaku could imagine the villagers stripping the red clothes off the pockmarked bodies. Before long he could see red things being handed down into the five little boats. There seemed to be a large quantity as the men passed them one after another to the waiting hands below. Finally, what appeared to be ship's tools were loaded into the boats before they pushed away from the side of the ship. The five boats threaded a path through the reef and made their way back to the shore, where the villagers were waiting by the water's edge. The bounty from the ship was unloaded and carried promptly to where the village chief was standing. Isaku had expected to be assailed by a nauseating stench from the pus-stained clothes, but there was nothing more than the dank smell of mold.

The elder spread out the clothes and, eyes agog with satisfaction, pronounced, "This is a good rugged cloth. And just look at this beautiful red." The belts and socks were also a vivid red, and it was quite beyond Isaku how something could be dyed to produce such a color. It was a far deeper hue, much finer in texture, and had a better sheen to it than anything in cloth woven from linden bark. Sighs of wonder could be heard from the women standing on the beach. Utensils claimed from the ship included a rice tray, some sacks of charcoal, a wooden brazier, some pots and pans, and a red monkey mask.

The village chief sneezed two or three times before leaving the beach accompanied by the more senior members of the community. The elder ordered the clothes and utensils to be carried to the chief's house. Several men tossed ropes into their boats and started rowing away from the shore, ten little vessels in all.

The boats pulled up alongside the ship on the reef, and the men on board tied the ropes firmly to the larger vessel. Using long poles, they worked hard to dislodge the ship from the rocks; finally it lurched free and floated clear. The fleet of little boats headed for the deeper water offshore, the ropes straining taut as the ship and its complement of corpses slowly drifted away from the shore. Isaku could still faintly hear the fishermen's rowing chant, though in the heavy snowfall he soon lost sight of the group of little boats.

The Hour of the Sheep came and went before the men returned from towing the ship out to sea. The snow had stopped. They knelt in front of the village chief and the elder and reported that they had towed the ship out far enough to see it taken by the current toward the northeast. The elder nodded. As a sign that prayers of gratitude for being blessed with the coming of O-fune-sama should begin, the village chief pressed his palms together. The villagers turned to face the sea and followed his lead. Weak shards of sunlight peeked from between the clouds, lighting up the sea far offshore.

When the village chief had finished his prayer, the elder said, "The clothes bestowed upon us by O-fune-sama shall be given to little girls and women. They will be handed out at the chief's house. None will be given to the men."

A hint of a titter could be detected from the men. The village chief and the elder headed off up the beach, followed by the villagers. No doubt Isaku's sister and mother would be given some of the clothes, and Isaku felt elated at the thought that their house would be brightened by the brilliant red.

The elders of the village walked into the chief's house proper, the rest of the throng remaining on the lower dirt floor. Folded up in neat sets, the red clothes were laid out in rows on the straw mats. The very sight of these garments brought grins of joy to the faces of the women.

Bowing deeply in front of the village chief, the senior elder got to his feet. "There are twenty-three sets of clothing. Counting from the smallest child, they will be given to twenty-three young girls. It wasn't clear how to divide up the socks and the belts, but our revered chief decided that since this red is also used to celebrate old age, we should give them to old women so that they might live longer, healthier lives yet, and so the belts and socks will be given out to the oldest among them," he said, surveying the scene in the room. When the elder sat down, three men got to their feet and stood beside the display of clothes. As one of them called out the name of a young girl, the other two, kneeling, picked up a set of clothes and held it beside the edge of the raised straw-matting section of the floor. The parents of the girls named came forward to receive their allotted garments. Some households were even given two or three sets. The grateful people prostrated themselves in front of the village chief.

On hearing the man announce the name of Isaku's younger sister, Kane, Isaku's mother stepped forward, accepted the clothes, and raised them above her head in a show of gratitude. Her eyes sparkled with joy, and a smile beamed across her face.

The belts and socks were handed out to the old women, some of whom smiled with embarrassment at receiving something so splendid. By now the cheerful atmosphere had infected everyone in the room.

When the last of the clothes had been handed out, the elder bowed deeply in front of the village chief before getting to his feet.

"The presentation of the bounty from O-fune-sama is over. These are truly fine garments, so use them only for celebrations. Take good care of them so that they may be passed down to generations to come. And remember, these clothes are from the bodies on O-fune-sama. Make sure to scrub them clean."

The villagers gathered in the room prostrated themselves on the floor in response to the elder's words. As soon as the women stepped out of the chief's house they broke into a lively chatter. They were not slow to realize that the adult clothes could be unstitched and made into two or even three pieces of clothing for a little girl. Laughter broke out among the old women when one of them wrapped a belt around herself like a loincloth. Isaku plodded back through the snow to his house, eyes focused on his mother, for the gaiety in her face was something he had not seen in a long time.

When they got back home, his mother placed the red clothes in front of the family's ancestral tablet and lit the small amount of oil she had poured into a wooden dish. Isokichi was cutting firewood down on the dirt floor and Kane was playing beside him, but when their mother beckoned, they came up onto the straw matting and sat in front of the ancestral tablet. Following their mother's lead, Isaku and his brother and sister raised their hands in prayer. The light in the little dish flickered as the dark of the night started to set in. Their mother scooped rice from the open bale and started to boil gruel. "The day your father gets back we'll dress you in some nice red clothes," she said to Kane as the little girl sipped on her vegetable porridge.

Isaku was once again reminded that their father never left his mother's thoughts. He could picture the scene next spring when the four of them, with Kane all dressed up in her red clothes, would go out to meet his father after his three years as a bond slave. In the murk of the room, the red clothes stood out in bold relief against the dim light from the dish but looked somehow out of place. Indeed, the inside of the house seemed to be glowing, with only that spot lit up.

The next morning when they awoke, the sea was calm, so Isaku and Isokichi got ready to go out fishing. Their mother was already washing the red clothes in the little stream behind the house. It seemed that other women were doing the same, because Isaku could hear their cheerful voices.

He pushed the boat out and dropped a line over the side once he got near the reef. Isokichi called out and motioned with a half turn of his head for Isaku to look to the shore. Isaku couldn't help smiling at the sight of bright red garments hanging out to dry throughout the village. The swaying objects were the belts, and the things that looked like red berries on a tree must have been the socks. With the snow-covered mountainside as a backdrop to the village, it was a beautiful sight to behold.

By the time they returned in the late afternoon, the bright red color had disappeared. Isaku swung the oar over his shoulder and made his way home with Isokichi.

The red clothes had been hung up on the wall. With the stains now washed off, the red appeared all the brighter and the material had a keen luster to it. The elder had said that the clothes should be stored with great care so that they might be handed on to future generations, and indeed they were so precious that chances were the village would never see anything like them again.

Isokichi, too, stood for some time in front of the garments, his eyes glistening in awe.

8

The village was still covered in deep snow, but the worst of the winter was over. Icicles that had been hanging from the eaves of the houses seemed to vanish in the space of a day, and a vaporous haze hung over the surface of the brook that flowed past Isaku's house. With the coming of February, sleet became more common.

According to his mother, some families had already taken the red garments apart, cut the cloth to their daughters' sizes and begun to sew their creations together. His mother could often be seen casting a contented glance from her daughter Kane to the red clothes hanging on the wall, comparing the size of one against the other.

The sea was calm for days on end, and the chill had left the air. Isaku's mother carefully unstitched the red clothes and cut the cloth to match Kane's body and arm measurements. Then she placed the cloth against her daughter before starting to sew the pieces together.

The first signs of spring came earlier than usual, and the snow covering the village started to melt. Large cracks appeared in the snow on the roofs, and before long it was sliding noisily to the ground. The village chief ordered the salt-making on the beach to stop.

When Isaku returned home from fishing the next evening, his mother told him that his cousin Takichi's daughter was running a high fever and was evidently in serious condition. Born late in January of the previous year, she had been growing at a prodigious rate, which of course was only to be expected with someone as sturdy as Kura for a mother. Recalling the sight of this hardy little girl often playing down on the sand while her mother combed the shore made it difficult to believe that she could fall ill.

"Some bad flus go around about the time the snow melts. Just because it gets a little warmer is no reason to walk around lightly dressed," his mother said as she checked whether the pot of gruel had come to a boil.

Sudden death was nothing unusual for infants in the village, and it was said that parents could not relax until their children had survived to see their fifth New Year. Most of the deaths occurred during winter, and the cold winds off the sea were blamed for many of the illnesses. Takichi's little daughter had often been down on the shore with Kura, so maybe that was why she fell ill.

The next day the sea was rough, and rather than put his boat out, Isaku made his way through the snow into the forest behind the village; he looked for fallen trees that he could drag back to the house and cut up for firewood. Isokichi lent a hand, but he complained of feeling listless and often stopped to rest.

Even with nightfall the wind showed no signs of letting

up, and the houses were enveloped in the sound of the waves crashing against the beach.

Isaku awoke just before dawn. He rolled over and snuggled deeper into his straw bedding but noticed that his covers were moving ever so slightly. He thought it must be the wind, but then he heard a groan so he poked his head out to take a look.

In the dim light of the fire Isaku could just make out Isokichi's face, the younger boy lying on his side as he slept. Isokichi had his eyes closed, but the straw covers on top of him were moving. Isaku could now hear Isokichi grinding his teeth, and he finally realized that it was the movement of Isokichi's covers that had been moving his own.

"Iso, what's the matter?" Isaku asked, peeking at his brother.

"It's so cold," said Isokichi, opening his eyes. His voice trembled, and the words faded away before he could finish them.

"It's not cold tonight. What's wrong?" Isaku straightened up Isokichi's covers, touching his brother's shoulder in the process. It felt wickedly hot, so Isaku placed his hand against Isokichi's forehead.

"You've got a fever all right."

"I can't stop shivering . . . and I have a terrible headache," said Isokichi, screwing up his face.

Isaku crawled out of bed and put some more wood on the fire.

"What's wrong?" His mother sat up. Isaku told her that Isokichi had a fever and a headache.

"I'm feverish, too. Feels like I've got the flu as well. Boil some water, I'll make some herb tea," she said, standing up and pulling a jacket over her shoulders as she stepped over to Isokichi. Isaku bent down over the bucket, breaking the thin layer of ice as he scooped out some water, then poured it into a pot which he placed on the fire. His mother wet a cloth with ice water and laid it on Isokichi's forehead.

Steam started to rise. Their mother stepped on the dirt floor to get some dried *shiso* leaves, which were hanging on the wall. She dropped them into the hot water and watched them spread out and then bob up and down as the water came to a boil. Isaku kept the fire going, but his eyes were riveted on his younger brother.

After a while their mother ladled some of the brown-colored concoction into a bowl, coaxed Isokichi into a sitting position, and made him drink. The boy was trembling so much that the bowl almost spilled, but grimacing, he managed to drink it all down before lying back.

His mother split open a pickled plum and rubbed it onto both sides of his forehead. "This'll take care of your headache by sunrise," she said as she drank some of the tea herself.

Isaku moved away from the fireside and snuggled back into his straw bedding. Shivering, he pulled his legs right up under the covers, but the bed had long since lost its warmth. He gazed at the flames in the fire and in no time had dropped off back to sleep.

Isaku woke up to the sound of crying. His mother was sitting beside Kane, who was weeping in a rasping, dry voice. The first dim light of dawn was filtering into the room.

The straw covers had stopped moving. Isaku turned his eyes toward his younger brother. Maybe the herb tea had worked and brought the boy's temperature down, thought Isaku, but Isokichi was now just lying there, breathing hard with his mouth half open. Isaku touched the boy's forehead. It was very hot. Isokichi had his eyes closed but didn't seem to be asleep.

Isaku got up and went over to the fire to warm his hands. "Kane's not well, is she?" he said to his mother.

"She's got an awful fever. But it's the headache that's making her cry," she replied, still with her back to him.

Isaku stood up and peered over his mother's shoulder at Kane. Her face was red and she was crying at the top of her lungs. It wasn't uncommon for influenza to spread quickly from house to house at the end of each winter, in some cases forcing every member of the family into their beds. But normally two or three days of rest and herb tea would lead to a complete recovery.

Isaku stepped onto the dirt floor and picked up a bundle of wood for the fire. Then, continuing his morning routine, he stepped outside and looked out to sea and then up at the sky. The wind had died down, with the stars mere specks of fading light above the barely visible horizon. By now the sea was much quieter, and the pale white of the foam was all that could be seen of the waves as they broke on the shore.

"How does the sea look?" asked Isaku's mother as she placed a pot on the fire.

"A lot calmer, but with Isokichi and Kane both sick . . ."

"You saying you're not going out? Leave them to me. What good's a fisherman who doesn't fish?" his mother snapped, irritated that two of the children had fallen ill on her.

Isaku started getting ready to go out in the boat.

That day he fished alone for the first time in a long while. Working the oar with one hand, he played the line with the other. He tried to copy the adult fishermen by moving the oar with his foot, but his lack of size made this difficult.

Around midday Isaku ate one of the millet dumplings he had wrapped in seaweed. He recognized a plume of snow dust rising into the air in the mountains behind the village, an indication that the avalanches had started. Most of the snow had already dropped off the roofs of the houses in the village. He thought that maybe this year the schools of sardines that always accompanied spring might appear inshore earlier than usual.

Hearing a voice behind him, Isaku turned around to see Sahei's boat approaching. He wrapped up the dumpling in the seaweed again.

Sahei pulled his boat alongside Isaku's and said, "Any of your family down with a fever?"

"Yes, Isokichi and Kane are both sick, and my mother said she's got a chill, too.

"I thought as much," he said dejectedly.

"Something wrong?" said Isaku, looking inquisitively at Sahei.

"Seems there's quite a few people with this fever. My sister's down with it. Didn't you notice how few boats there are out today? Can only mean that either the man's sick or someone in his family's down with it."

Isaku looked around as Sahei spoke. He had thought that the slight swell might have been why so few people were out . . . but then again, normally there probably would be a good number of boats out on a sea like this.

"There aren't many out, that's for sure. It's a wicked flu, this one," said Isaku in whispered tones.

"You all right?" asked Sahei as he looked across the water.

"I'm fine."

"Well, let's both be careful we don't get it. That wind off the sea can really give it to you. Once the sun goes down the wind turns icy. Best to head in early, I reckon," Sahei said as he grasped his oar and started to work his little boat forward.

Isaku thought how considerate his friend was as he watched the gap between their two boats widen. Sahei may have had an obstinate side to him, but time had seen him become more mild mannered, and his attitude toward Isaku reflected the feeling of brotherhood shared by men working on the sea. There was still much to learn from Sahei, thought Isaku.

He finished eating and started fishing again.

When the sun began to go down, he turned the prow of the little boat toward shore. Partly because of Sahei's advice, but also because he wanted to get back home quickly to see how everyone was. There wasn't a soul to be seen gathering shellfish or seaweed on the shore, an eerie reminder of Sahei's comment that many people had fallen ill.

He pulled the boat onto shore and headed for his house, oar on one shoulder and the basket holding his catch on the other. His long shadow moved across the sand and up the path to the village.

As he entered the house, he looked toward the middle of the room and was surprised to see his mother lying on her side, too.

"Are you all right?" Isaku asked.

"I'm burning up. . . . But I feel cold all over. I just can't stay on my feet," she said through parched lips.

Isaku thought it was just as well he had come back early, not only to look after his sick family but to get the housework done. He went out the back door and filled a bucket with water from the brook, scooping some snow into it to make sure it was cold. When he got back indoors, he put pieces of cloth in the water, wrung them out, and carefully placed one first on his mother's forehead, then on Isokichi's and Kane's. He boiled up some herbal tea, put a good measure of rice into a pot, and made some gruel. He'd heard that rice was good for curing illnesses, so this was no time to be stingy with their supply.

Both Isokichi and Kane complained of headaches, and the little girl was crying in a rasping voice. The pieces of cloth soon become warm, so Isaku dropped them back into the ice water every few minutes.

During the night he woke up often to tend to his family. His mother was breathing heavily. The next day their fevers got worse, and they started to complain of back pain as well. Their mother seemed to be in particular distress, pressing her hand against her back and clenching her teeth. Isaku stayed at home rather than go out on the water in his boat.

Just after midday, without warning, the elder appeared at the door with two other men. He frowned at the sight of Isaku's mother lying prone on the straw matting.

Isaku stepped down onto the dirt floor and knelt in front of the elder.

"So your family's come down with it, too? When did the fever start?" he asked, watching Isaku's mother.

"Early yesterday morning for my brother and sister, and yesterday afternoon for my mother."

"You're all right I see."

Isaku replied that he was well.

"It's a wicked flu, this one. The chief is down with a fever, too. An exorcism of the demons that caused this affliction is being performed in the chief's house, so make sure you set up a light offering in front of your family's ancestral tablet."

The message was well rehearsed, as though the elder was going around making the same announcement to all the households. After casting his eyes back once more toward Isaku's ailing family, he left the house followed by the other two men.

Isaku stepped back up onto the straw-matted area and set up a light offering in front of their ancestral tablet. Based on what the elder had said, most of the villagers must be suffering from the same ailment. Even so, Isaku would never have imagined that the village chief would come down with it.

The sound of the water flowing in the brook had increased over the last few days. Signs of spring were everywhere, and surely, Isaku thought, with this would come an end to the affliction plaguing the village.

But the next day his mother's fever worsened and she began to groan in pain. The pain in her back had intensified, and she pleaded with Isaku to do something to relieve it. For someone as strong-willed as his mother to be saying this could only be proof she was in agony. Isaku busied himself keeping a steady supply of cold, wet cloths and herb tea.

Whether it was the tea's taking effect or that they had simply passed the worst of it he didn't know, but the next morning Isokichi, Kane, and their mother all seemed to be running less of a fever. Their headaches and back pain seemed to have subsided, and all three had stopped groaning. They looked completely exhausted, but relieved.

While Isaku was pleased with the apparent improvement in their condition, he noticed that their puffy faces seemed to be covered with something like a heat rash. The little spots gradually reddened, and by evening they had spread to their arms, legs, back, and chest.

When Isaku woke up the next morning, he was shocked at the sight of their faces. Realizing that the change in Isokichi and Kane was also occurring in herself, their mother tilted her head to one side and ran her fingers across her own face.

"Maybe the fever's caused this rash," she said skeptically as she gazed at Isokichi and Kane.

It was the first day in some time that they'd awakened to the sound of a strong wind, and the thunder of the waves breaking against the shore weighed on them heavily.

Isaku had no idea why they had broken out in a rash like this. He knew that there were all sorts of symptoms with influenza, so he simply thought that perhaps this one included a rash. Since the spots had appeared after the fever went down, Isaku presumed that this must be a sign of recovery. With the fever abating, they managed to sit up to eat the midday meal Isaku had made. But it was clear that the high temperature for several days running had taken its toll. Even the act of sitting up looked painful, and almost the moment they put their bowls down, they lay back again and closed their eyes. Isaku stared at his mother's face as she started to take the long audible breaths of someone drifting into sleep. The spots had swollen to a considerably larger size than they had been that morning, and each one seemed full of a clear fluid. The same change was now apparent in Isokichi and Kane.

The straw matting at the front entrance of the house moved slightly. Isaku stepped onto the dirt floor and across to the entrance to see the village chief's manservant standing outside.

"I've heard that some of your family are sick. Do they have boils on their faces?" he asked.

"They're not what you'd call boils, more like a sort of heat rash . . ."

"So they do have them. Anyway, come straight down to

the beach. Our revered elder has something important to say," said the manservant in hurried tones before he scuttled off to the next house.

As Isaku put out the fire, he thought that from what the chief's manservant had said, his family was not the only one to have broken out in a rash. If most of the people in the village had come down with the fever at the same time, and if they were all now afflicted with the rash, then it obviously had spread very quickly and must be extremely contagious. Isaku thought that the reason for getting the remaining healthy people together on the beach could only be to advise them of the best way to treat their ailing family members.

Isaku put on his shoes and stepped outside. The wind was strong, but he didn't feel cold. The ground was starting to appear in places through the snow on the path. A group of men and women were sitting around the little hut near the salt cauldrons on the beach, with the elder standing in the middle. Isaku got down on his knees and bowed deeply in front of the old man.

Isaku noticed a very old man sitting next to the elder. The old man's name was Jinbei; Isaku remembered seeing him several years earlier shuffling along with a walking stick. The old man's health had further deteriorated, and evidently he had been bedridden since the last time Isaku had seen him. For many years he had worked as the village chief's right-hand man, but advancing age had make him relinquish the position to the present senior elder. Now he was frail, his white hair thinned to no more than a few strands, his toothless mouth gaping. Isaku could not for the life of him understand why old Jinbei should be down there on the beach with them.

Sensing that there was something out of the ordinary in

Jinbei's presence, the villagers sat waiting tensely. "It looks like everyone's here. This is important, so listen carefully. Jinbei says that the illness that has stricken the village may not be influenza after all. That it might be a plague far worse than that. Jinbei was so concerned that despite his difficulties he has gone out of his way to talk to us," said the elder in a grave tone, bowing his head to Jinbei.

With this, Jinbei attempted to get to his feet, and two young men stepped forward to lift him to a standing position. His sunken eyes opened wide as he stood there trembling.

"When I went to the next village long ago, when I was young, I stayed in a place where I met a man from far off. I asked him how he got the terrible pockmarks on his face, and he told me that they were from smallpox. He said that small-pox was very contagious and that after suffering from high fevers, spots would appear all over your body. It drove some people mad, he said. And even if you lived through the disease, you could be covered by hideous pockmarks. It sounded like such an awful disease that I can remember his words to this day."

Just saying that much made Jinbei gasp for breath.

Isaku shuddered with fear but thought surely this couldn't be the same thing. While his family did have spots all over them, the fever had gone down and they seemed to be over the worst of the illness. With them showing what appeared to be the first signs of recovery, it was unthinkable that any of them might go mad or die.

"I asked the man if there was any medicine that could cure the disease, and he said no. He said that the only thing was to pray and to wear something red. When I heard that the bodies on *O-fune-sama* were wearing red, I didn't think of smallpox, but when someone said that there was a red monkey mask on the ship, I thought again. Smallpox is a disease that is passed from human to human, so maybe the monkey mask was used to ward off the illness. I think the fact that the bodies on board were wearing red clothes proves that they had smallpox. The thought haunts me," said Jinbei in a piercing voice as he slumped back down to the ground.

The villagers were unmoved and remained sitting impassively on the sand. Isaku remembered the monkey mask. It was only natural that a monkey's face should be red, but it was indeed strange that the eyes and the rest of the head should be red, too. Maybe it was to ward off disease, as Jinbei suggested.

The senior elder stood silent for a time before speaking out in a grave voice.

"If Jinbei is right, then that ship wasn't O-fune-sama. Maybe there had been an outbreak of this plague called smallpox in some town or village, and they decided to put all those who had come down with it on a ship and send them away to stop the disease from spreading. The people on board died while the ship was drifting at sea, and eventually it ran onto the rocks in front of us. It's possible that we took clothes that carried the poison and that our people were infected. Our chief asked whether we'd be safe taking clothes soiled by the boils on the bodies, but it was me who said there was no need to worry. If this is smallpox rather than a flu, then I'm to blame for everything," agonized the elder.

A painful silence spread through the gathering on the beach.

"What should we do?" asked one of the men in a subdued voice.

Neither Jinbei nor the senior elder said anything, both avoiding the man's eyes.

Isaku quietly watched for any change in the symptoms of his sick family. That day and the next their fever continued to ease, but the spots increased in number, spreading to cover all of their arms, legs, neck, chest, and back. Isaku's mother and the two sick children seemed listless and had no appetite. Whether or not his mother was relying on Isaku's help to get her through the day he didn't know, but even on days when the sea was calm she didn't urge him to go out on the water. Isaku busied himself making tea for them and wiping the sweat from their bodies.

As the sun started to set in the west, the straw matting covering the entrance to their house opened slightly to reveal the village chief's manservant peeking in. The man beckoned to Isaku, who stepped straight down onto the dirt floor and walked outside. The senior elder was standing there with two men at his side.

The old man asked anxiously about Isaku's family. Isaku told him that the fever had gone down, that he thought they were getting better.

"What about the spots?" asked the elder, intently studying Isaku's expression.

"There's more of them. They're worst on their faces. They're on their mouths, noses, and even inside their ears."

The elder nodded. The somber look on his face was an indication that the other villagers were suffering from the same symptoms.

"I'd just like to ask, if this sickness is contagious, will I get it, too, by taking care of them? Their fevers are going down, so I don't see how it can be the horrible disease you talk about."

Isaku thought that the elder's grave expression looked exaggerated.

"Jinbei said that with all hideous diseases, one of every three people dies, one survives, and one doesn't come down with it at all. That mankind is never wiped out by disease, he says, is due to the benevolence of the gods. If that's the case, then there's nothing strange about you or me not coming down with it," said the elder in a voice that was little more than a whisper. As the other men began to move away, he stepped back toward the path through the village.

Isaku went back inside the house and sat down by the fire. Kane was restless, but their mother was sleeping soundly. Isaku had no idea what condition the other villagers were in, but at least his family seemed to be finally on the road to recovery.

Isaku stepped onto the dirt floor to start the evening meal.

For the next two days their fever continued to drop, but on the evening of the third day Isaku was in despair at the thought that the elder's misgivings seemed to be coming true. The fever returned with a vengeance, and the spots became much more densely clustered on their skin.

Kane vomited again and again, wailing and crying in between attacks. Their mother and Isokichi moaned in agony with the latest bouts of headache and backache, and when Isaku touched their foreheads, he was amazed at how hot they were.

The next morning he was horrified when he saw their faces in the clear sunlight shining into the house. The spots had changed to a yellow color and seemed to have all burst at once, leaving a suppurating mass oozing down their faces. Their eyes were blocked with pus, but lacking the strength to wipe it away, the three of them just lay there gasping for air.

Isaku finally understood that this was no ordinary illness and could only be the disease called smallpox that Jinbei had described. Yet rather than having a disease, it looked as if they had been cursed. Even the word "pox" had an eerie ring to it.

His mother and Isokichi groaned desperately as Kane cried in a rasping voice between violent muscle spasms. Giving them herb tea was obviously having no effect, and Isaku now had no idea how he should be treating them.

Gripped by panic, he rushed out of the house and ran down to the beach. Maybe the elder would be holding a meeting there; but not a soul was to be seen, so he headed for the village chief's house, hoping to get some advice to help his family.

On the way up the slope to the village chief's house, Isaku saw a dozen or so men and women standing in the yard, all deathly pale.

"There's pus all over their faces," Isaku shouted as he ran toward the villagers.

"My family's the same. All the sick ones are covered in pus," said a middle-aged man in a trembling voice.

The elder came out of the chief's house. His white-whiskered face looked gaunt, and his eyes were bloodshot. He looked around the congregation and in a feeble voice said, "Jinbei was right. It must be smallpox. The chief's eyes are blocked up with pus, too."

"What can we do to make it easier for them?" asked one man imploringly.

"We can do nothing but pray," he replied, his head bowed as he left the yard and moved unsteadily down the slope.

The village was in an uproar. The symptoms of most of the sick people were more or less the same, and by all accounts many were losing their minds. Kane was clearly insane, launching herself again and again into a bolt-upright sitting position as she wailed in a strange high-pitched voice, something between laughter and crying. After each attack Isaku lay her back down on her straw bedding.

The next morning he heard that several people had died during the night. Kane's condition continued to deteriorate, and after a series of violent fits around midday, she, too, died. Their mother and Isokichi had both lost consciousness, so neither was aware of what had happened.

The following day the elder left a note in his house and then jumped to his death from the cliffs near Crow Point. The waves smashed his body onto the rocks again and again, his head to pieces. The note was addressed to the village chief. It recorded the elder's deepest apologies for bringing this terrible disease into the village by his declaration that the pus-stained red clothes were safe to wear, and explained how he had chosen to take his own life to atone for his misjudgment.

The elder's son was given the task of collecting the body and disposing of it in deep water. Suicide was judged a sinful act, so the custom was for the culprit's body to be dropped into the sea rather than to be given an honorable burial on land.

With the elder's death, the village was further cast into turmoil. The number of deaths increased dramatically, and with no indication of how the bodies should be disposed of, the surviving family members could do little but set up a light offering to the gods and pray in front of the family shrine. There was no way enough coffins could be built to handle the number of dead, so the bodies were left in the houses.

Eventually, at Jinbei's instructions, two men went around the village and told the people what to do with the bodies. Because there weren't enough able-bodied people to carry so many bodies up to the crematory, they were told that the next day the bodies should be burned on the beach and the bones carried up for burial the day after.

Isaku wrapped Kane's body in some straw matting and carried her outside. There was no change in either his mother's or Isokichi's condition; both of them lay unconscious, gasping feverishly for air.

Isaku made a funeral pyre out of a crisscross arrangement of pieces of wood and lay Kane's body on top. He worked some kindling until it caught fire and the wood started to burn. The straw matting soon burned away to expose his sister's face engulfed in flames; no tears came into Isaku's eyes. Around him were little groups of villagers standing beside their own flaming pyres. They all looked intent on burning away the virulence harbored by the bodies of their loved ones, and all seemed to have forgotten the sorrow of losing a family member.

While there were many infants and young children among the dead, there also were a number of young men and women and old people. Isaku fed the fire with wood and poked at Kane's body with a bamboo rod to make sure the flames burned their way through.

At dusk Isaku picked up the bones and put them in a wooden tub. There was hardly anything to them.

When he got home, he placed the tub in front of the

ancestral tablet and started to grill a fish on the fire. He called out to his mother and Isokichi, urging them to have something to eat, but they just lay there gasping, incapable of uttering a word in reply. Their mouths and nostrils were full of clotted pus.

That night a squall blew up and covered the house in sheets of rain. The downpour stopped by morning, but the house creaked with the force of the wind.

Isaku passed time quietly tending to his mother and Isokichi. Their arms, legs, and faces swelled even more, and fresh pus oozed from under what had already caked onto their skin, which by now was invisible under the purulent mass. It was as if they were wearing masks.

Jinbei's messengers called again, this time advising that recovery would begin once the scabs fell off naturally, and not to remove them prematurely. Isaku did his best to feed his mother and Isokichi, spooning gruel into their mouths through the gap between their scab-encrusted lips.

Day after day corpses were being burned on the beach. Uneasy, Isaku went down to the shore to help carry firewood. It seemed that the village chief was still alive but in serious condition.

The weather grew warmer and calm days with mist rising off the sea more frequent. The snow disappeared from the slopes behind the village, the only remaining traces of winter the sparkling strips of white on the distant ridges.

The beach was covered with the blackened charcoal remains of funeral pyres, some still burning. The number of bodies being burned was falling, an indication that the pestilence was on the wane.

When Isaku awoke one day early in March, he noticed that the scab covering his mother's right eye had dried up and fallen off. The eye was looking his way. The scabs covering the mouth moved and a muffled voice leaked out. "Kane's dead, isn't she?"

Isaku nodded, replying, "Many people have died."

His mother quietly closed her eyes.

That night both his mother and Isokichi started wailing. The itchiness under the scabs was unremitting, and unable to scratch for fear of worsening their condition, all they could do to get some relief was to press down on the dried pus.

The next day, while the urge to scratch at the scabs was still there, the fever had gone down somewhat. At the same time the caked mass that had covered their legs and arms was beginning to flake off. Pus no longer oozed out from under the scabs on their faces, and a pale powdery substance spread over their skin.

No more funeral pyres were lit on the beach. The itchiness that had tormented Isaku's mother and Isokichi gradually let up, and the scabs on their faces curled up, ready to fall off. Isaku told them it would be best to let the scabs fall off naturally, but his mother couldn't bear them on her face any longer and started to pick at them with her finger. Nothing adverse happened as a result, and in no time they were even able to eat again unaided. The spots on the skin where the scabs had been were strangely white, with a reddish depression marking the place where the boil had been.

Isaku finally realized that his mother and Isokichi had recovered, but he shuddered when he heard Isokichi say, "I can't see anything." Star-shaped bulges covered the pupil of each eye.

His mother and Isokichi would get out of bed and sit by the fire, mostly without saying a word. As the days passed, the red color faded where the boils had been, but pockmarks were left not just on their faces but all over their necks, shoulders, arms, and legs.

Reluctant to leave Kane's bones sitting in the house, Isaku put them in a pot and set off up the hill to the crematory, where he buried them. Beside him an old woman was swinging a hoe as she dug a hole to bury the bones of two dead kin.

A few days later all the people who had not been infected by the disease were summoned to assemble on the beach. Isaku dropped what he was doing and went straight to the shore. About thirty men and women were standing in front of the little hut used in tending the salt cauldrons. He saw how few people had survived unscathed and realized how badly the village had been ravaged by the disease.

Isaku's eyes scanned the faces in the crowd. Sahei was there, but no sign of Tami.

The village chief arrived down the slope to the beach sitting in a makeshift litter shouldered by four men. The pockmarks covering his face served as a graphic reminder of what he had been through. As the villagers prostrated themselves, Jinbei's son Manbei stepped forward and knelt before the chief as the litter was set down on the sand. They spoke in whispers before Manbei nodded his assent and turned around to address the villagers.

"It is the command of our revered chief that I take up the position of elder in the village. We have been stricken by a most terrible calamity, but the disease has now passed. The chief has decided what we must do. Those still keeping the bones of dead family members in their houses should see to it that they are taken up to the crematory and buried as soon as possible. Also, most of you will be spending your time taking care of your family, but those of you who can should be out fishing or collecting shellfish on shore or tilling the soil. Now let us join our chief in a prayer to the sea."

With this Manbei sat down beside the village chief.

The chief pressed his hands together in prayer, and the assembled followed as they turned to look out to sea. Isaku heard the sound of sobbing and felt tears welling in his own eyes. The grief over Kane's death that he hadn't felt until now suddenly overcame him. His heart bled for his little sister when he thought that her last moments of life were spent thrashing like a fish on a boat's deck.

That day a good number of villagers could be seen heading up the hill to the crematory, carrying boxes or bags holding the bones of their loved ones. Isaku caught sight of Tami's father limping his way up the path, a box in his arms. The thought that it might contain Tami's bones sent a shiver down Isaku's spine.

The next day the sea was rough, but the following morning Isaku put his boat out for the first time in a while. The star-shaped blotches on Isokichi's eyes were still dark and the blindness showed no signs of improvement. Even blind, Isokichi might somehow manage to work the oar, but it would be impossible for him to go out on a boat for some time.

Before long the sardines started to bite, so much so that no sooner would Isaku drop the hook in the water than he would be pulling up a shimmering fish on the line. Other boats seemed to be having the same success.

They grilled the day's catch over the fire for their evening meal.

"The peach trees'll probably be coming into flower up in the mountains now," whispered his mother as she took a sardine to eat.

Isaku studied his mother's expression. He was reminded

that before long his father would return home. In the three years his father had been away both Teru and Kane had died, and now Isokichi had lost his sight. Their father would be grief-stricken, so their mother was probably more fearful than happy at the prospect of seeing him again. And on top of that, as a wife she was no doubt mortified at the prospect of showing her hideously scarred face to her husband.

Isokichi sat there with a look of despair on his face, but their mother began to work around the house. When she went outside, she wrapped a cloth around her cheeks to hide as much as she could of her face. The women Isaku passed on the path were similarly self-conscious, using either a scarf to conceal their faces or wearing sedge hats with the brim pulled down low.

Isaku saw several women on the shore and noticed that Tami was among them. He flushed with excitement at the thought that she had survived. She had a scarf wrapped around her face and was wearing a sedge hat on her head, proof that her face must be covered with pockmarks.

Little by little the names of those claimed by the disease became known. In Isaku's cousin Takichi's family, the child died and Takichi lost his sight. Isaku saw his cousin being led by the hand by Kura, the brim of her sedge hat pulled down low over her face. Isaku's mother put some dried sardines in a bamboo basket and took them to Takichi's house.

As the moon started to wane toward the end of the month, after nightfall one day, the droning of the sutras punctuated by the ringing of a bell could be heard from the village chief's house. At first Isaku was taken aback, thinking that someone in the village chief's family must have died, maybe even the chief himself, but on rushing up to the house he saw the chief and Manbei the elder, kneeling and chanting.

Jinbei was there, too, sitting to one side, leaning against a pile of straw mats.

Isaku assumed they must be praying to celebrate the defeat of demons that had brought the disease to the village, so he returned home to set up a light offering in front of the family's ancestral tablet.

But the sutras did not stop that evening. They continued for days on end, from sunset until late into the night. It seemed that Jinbei, Manbei, and the other senior villagers were actually sleeping at the chief's house, ringing the bell and chanting the sutras during their waking hours.

Isaku put a handful of rice into a bowl and placed it on the veranda of the village chief's house before joining the men in prayer. There was something strange about the atmosphere in the room. The chief and his entourage were chanting the sutras and fiercely sounding the bell, the manic cast to their bloodshot eyes making them look to all the world as if they were possessed. To a man their voices were hoarse and tired.

On a night when the moon had waned to a mere sliver of light the shape of a fishhook, a message went around that everyone except the lame and the very young were to gather in the village chief's courtyard. Isaku hurried along, flaming torch in hand, lighting the way for his mother as she led Isokichi by the hand. Torches emerged from the houses, converging at the path leading up the slope before gathering in the chief's courtyard. Once assembled, they extinguished their torches and knelt in the flickering light of the firebrands stuck into the ground in each corner of the yard.

Isaku thought that they would likely be offering prayers of gratitude for the return of tranquillity to the village. An air of solemn expectation hung over the villagers as they knelt in the courtyard. The village chief appeared from inside the house and sat on the veranda. Still on their knees, the villagers bowed down until their heads almost touched the ground.

Isaku straightened up and looked at the chief's face. The light of the flaming torches revealed the old man's features covered with hideous pockmarks.

Next, Jinbei emerged from the house, supported on one side by his son Manbei and on the other by an attendant; they half dragged him to where the chief was sitting. The villagers again bowed deeply.

"Listen carefully to what I have to say. The only thing for smallpox is banishment into the mountains. Those tainted with the disease can't stay among us in the village, they've got to go. Even if they have survived the disease, if they stay here, the poison lurking in them would someday come out to infect the healthy." Jinbei started to weep. His body trembled as the tears streamed down his face, glistening in the light of the torches.

Isaku cringed at Jinbei's announcement but could not comprehend the old man's words. Jinbei lifted his head and spoke again. "It pains me greatly to talk of banishing people. But if we don't, the poison will remain in the village and the demons of the disease will reappear to plague us again. In the end, everyone would die and the village would disappear. For the good of the village, I decided that I had to bring this up with our chief. I was afraid to mention it to our revered chief, as he himself has been afflicted by the disease and bears the ravages of the plague on his face. But the chief did not hesitate. . . ." With this Jinbei let out a wail and collapsed to the ground. Tears were now flowing down Manbei's cheeks, too, but he took up from where his father had left off.

"Our chief has said . . . letting the village perish would be an inexcusable sin against our ancestors . . . and he has said . . . he will go up into the mountains," said Manbei, stumbling on his words.

Isaku froze. It dawned on him that the chanting of the sutras and the ringing of the bells in the chief's house had been part of the prayers to prepare for banishment to the mountains.

Could banishment, thought Isaku, mean spending the rest of one's days away from the village, up in the mountains? There were mountain vegetables to be gathered, and birds and animals to be caught for food, but this would never be enough to survive on, and starvation would not be far away. Leaving the village to go into the mountains could only lead to death.

Isaku was panic-stricken. He was the only one in his family who hadn't come down with the disease, and as carriers of the smallpox poison, his mother and Isokichi would now have to leave. The villagers suddenly were agitated. Some looked at each other in disbelief; others, still incapable of grasping the situation, stared at the village chief and Manbei standing before them.

Isaku couldn't bring himself to look at his mother and Isokichi sitting beside him. The mere thought of it terrified him.

The sound of faint whispers arose from among the villagers, growing in volume until it reached a clamor. "This is awful." "We have to leave you." Isaku heard voices around him tinged with fear.

"Revered elder." The sad voice of a young man was heard.

Manbei turned his head slightly in the direction of the voice.

"Those who go into the mountains will not be able to come back, will they?"

Manbei nodded. The young man was momentarily lost for words but then spoke again.

"If they go into the mountains, they'll die of starvation. Can they not go to the next village or another village far away?"

"No. If the blight is taken into another village, smallpox will break out there, too. Our people contracted smallpox from the red clothes brought here off the ship. We can't pass it on to others outside our village," said Manbei firmly, tears streaming down his face.

Isaku couldn't bear the thought of parting with his mother and Isokichi and wanted to go up into the mountains with them. Stifled sobbing could now be heard from the crowd.

Manbei spoke again, his voice faltering.

"Our revered chief had read the sutras to prepare himself for leaving. Now that he has readied himself . . . to rid the village of the poison within us he must leave as quickly as possible and will depart at dawn tomorrow, at the Hour of the Tiger."

The sobbing increased in intensity.

"Come into the mountains with me," said the chief in a childlike voice before getting to his feet and disappearing into the house. The villagers bowed low.

"Return to your homes and get ready to leave. You have until the Hour of the Tiger to say your farewells. But remember, no one is to step outside to see anyone off," said Manbei in a powerful voice.

The villagers feebly got to their feet and trudged, heads down, out of the courtyard and along the path down the gentle slope. Illuminated by the faintest sliver of moon, the night sky was bristling with stars. The sea was calm, with the pale white ripple of each wave folding onto the shore barely perceptible in the dark of the night.

Their mother was the first to enter the house, walking ahead of her sons as she led Isokichi by the hand. She lit the fire and sat Isokichi down beside it before sitting down in front of the family's ancestral tablet to pray.

Sobbing, Isaku squatted down on the dirt floor. He wanted to go into the mountains with his mother and Isokichi, but he knew that would go against the village decree. He thought he'd rather die than be separated from his mother and Isokichi.

"Isaku, don't cry," he heard his mother say calmly.

Isaku sat there, his head in his hands.

His mother stepped down onto the dirt floor, scooped some rice from the open bale, and put it into a pot.

"The chief is going with us. It'll be all right. Teru's dead, and now Kane, too. I didn't want to be here to see your father come back to this. It's better this way. I feel sorry for Isokichi, though, being so young, but he's carrying the poison, too, so he has to accept it," she said in a voice little more than a whisper as she put another piece of wood on the fire.

The Hour of the Tiger was not far away, Isaku thought, and his mother and Isokichi were to leave the village. That was now irrevocable. The only thing left was to make the most of the short time they had left.

He got to his feet, stepped onto the matting floor, and sat down by the fire. Reaching out, he grasped Isokichi's hand. There was no reaction from his brother, who sat there still as a statue.

The grains of rice leaped in the hot water, but before long they, too, quieted down and the rice was ready to eat.

"I won't be able to cook him much, but I want to help

look after the chief for a month or so if I can. And I'll need food to do that. . . ."

Their mother shaped the cooked rice with her hands and wrapped it in seaweed. Then she bundled up some dried sardines in bamboo leaves and scooped five *shō* of rice from the open bale into a cloth bag.

Isaku carefully followed his mother's movements. Strangely, there was no trace of sadness on her pockmarked face. Her eyes were clear and determined, and there was even the hint of a contented smile on her lips.

She picked up the red clothes lying in the corner of the dirt floor and went outside through the back door. Isaku peered out after her. She lit some firewood and spread the clothes on top. Flames rose playfully.

The stars had changed their position in the sky, and by now the moon was hidden behind the treetops. The Hour of the Tiger was approaching.

Back inside the house, their mother paused for a short prayer in front of the ancestral tablet before busying herself with the final preparation for departure. The bag of rice went onto her back, and the cooked rice wrapped in seaweed was lashed with twine onto Isokichi's carrying frame, along with the dried fish bundled in the bamboo leaves. Lighting a firebrand, she led Isokichi by the hand.

"Be good to your father," his mother said, her eyes glistening for the first time. She and Isokichi left the house.

Isaku watched from the doorway as the two walked off by the light of their flaming torches. He traced the lights making their way down the village path until they became indistinguishable from those approaching from the opposite side. The group could be seen moving in the direction of the village chief's house until they disappeared from sight behind a large rock beside the path.

Isaku stood waiting. Before long the line of torches reappeared at the foot of the path leading into the mountains, swaying its way up the slope. It was a long but ever-shrinking line, as the rearmost lights approached and then disappeared into the forest, taking with it not only his mother and Isokichi but also Tami and his cousin Takichi.

The first signs of daybreak appeared in the starry sky.

Isaku spent the next day not knowing what to do with himself.

Several days later Manbei came to the house and told him to go out fishing. It seemed that Manbei was calling on everyone, worried that the remaining villagers were not attending to their work.

The first time Isaku put his boat out was at the end of March. The rain that had fallen steadily for two days had stopped and the sky was a clear blue, but the wind was gusting so there was a swell on the sea. No sign of sardines to be hooked, but Isaku didn't care. He just hung the line over the side as he maneuvered the little boat forward. Occasionally there was a fleeting glimmer of an agitated mass of silver scales below the surface.

Isaku heard a voice behind him and turned to see a man gesturing to the shore. Isaku looked in that direction.

His jaw dropped and he felt himself stiffen. Coming down the mountain path that led to the pass he saw a man; he was just about to disappear behind the trees along the sides of the path down the slope. Judging from his gait and build, there was no doubt it was Isaku's father. No one else was due to be coming down the mountain path at that time of year.

The man reappeared from the trees. He was walking steadily, without the use of a stick, carrying a small bag in his hand.

Isaku felt overwhelmed. He felt sorry for his father coming home to find their mother gone. The thought of the shock and pain when his father heard that only Isaku had survived cut the boy to the quick.

He wanted to turn his boat out to sea and let the currents take him away.

The power drained from Isaku's body and his head felt empty. An indescribable groan erupted from his throat. He grasped the oar and turned his boat back to the shore.